MAN BENEATH THE UNIFORM
by
Maureen Child

MAUREEN CHILD

is a California native who loves to travel. Every chance they get, she and her husband are taking off on another research trip. The author of more than sixty books, Maureen loves a happy ending and still swears that she has the best job in the world. She lives in Southern California with her husband, two children and a golden retriever with delusions of grandeur.

Visit her website at www.maureenchild.com.

To my mum, Sallye Carberry—
for the laughs, the support and always, the love.
I love you, Mum!

One

Zack Sheridan scowled at the streetlights shining through the wide window, then glared at the man sitting opposite him in the booth.

"She studies *fish?*" Danny Akiona, a full-blooded Hawaiian and a Navy SEAL, looked at his friend and laughed.

Irritating as hell, Zack told himself. Especially since, if the shoe had been on the other foot and it was Danny facing this assignment, Zack would be the one laughing.

Zack took another long swallow of his beer. But even the crisp bite of the alcohol couldn't quite take the sting out of his friend's laughter. Leaning back in the red leather booth, he turned to look at the crowd filling the waterfront bar.

Couples sat in booths and singles prowled the edges of the mob, looking to catch someone's— anyone's—eye. Music blared from an ancient juke- box loaded with everything from golden oldies to hip-hop. The waitresses, decked out in skintight, black leather miniskirts, red, belly-baring halter tops and red spike heels, dipped and swayed through the crowd, balancing trays full of drinks.

Zack sighed as he checked out an especially ap- pealing blond barmaid with a size forty chest packed into a size thirty-four top. If he'd been a free man, he'd have made a play for her and en- joyed his first night of leave. But since he was facing thirty days of pure hell, he just didn't have the heart for it.

"Oh, man." Danny chuckled and shook his head. "This is just too funny."

Zack shot him a look hot enough to cook bacon. "I'm glad somebody's getting a laugh out of this."

"It's perfect, man." Danny's dark brown eyes glittered with humor and his perpetually tanned face split into a wide grin. "We get a month's R and R and *you* get sentenced to baby-sit a sci- entist." He lifted his beer in a toast. "Here's to the women I'll get now that you're out of action for a while."

He'd be out of action, all right, Zack thought

miserably. Thirty long days of riding herd on some babe born with a silver spoon in her mouth and a yen to play with fish.

"Gonna be a long month." Zack shifted a glance out the front window of the bar to the bustling street beyond the glass.

Even on a chilly February evening, Savannah was crawling with tourists. With cameras slung around their necks and guidebooks clutched like the Bible, visitors wandered narrow streets and the waterfront. Gift shops did a bumper business year round and the locals tidily counted their pennies and waited for summer, when even *bigger* crowds would show up.

Savannah was a small Southern town disguised as a bustling city. It had a great harbor, beautiful old homes and a couple of really terrific bars. Ordinarily, Zack would be looking forward to a little down time here. He'd be wandering the town looking to pick up a couple of Southern belles. But this trip was all business.

Or punishment, rather.

"It's no surprise, man," Danny said, bringing Zack's attention back to the matter at hand. "Hell, you knew you'd have your ass kicked the minute we got back home."

Zack moved his glass through the water rings it had left on the highly varnished wood table. Glancing at his friend, he asked, "So, do you think I should have done it differently?"

"Hell, no." Danny straightened up in the red leather seat and leaned both forearms on the table-top. "If you hadn't gone back for Hunter..." His voice trailed off and he shook his head. "Unacceptable. No way. We had to go back for him. Orders or not."

"Hoo-yah." They lifted their glasses and clinked them together.

Zack nodded to himself. He knew he'd done the right thing—the *only* thing he could have done. But it was good to hear his friend back him up on it. The rules were simple and he lived by them. A Navy SEAL didn't leave a man behind. If a team of six men went in, then six men had better damn well come back out. Dead or alive, every SEAL *always* came home.

Memories rushed through his brain. Instants, moments, rose up, were recognized and then faded into the next. He remembered it all clearly. That mission two weeks before had gone bad from the beginning. His team had been sent in to infiltrate, rescue, then exit, fast.

But someone had screwed up the intel. The hostage wasn't where he was supposed to be. By the time Zack and the others had found their man, time was short. With only a couple of hours left before extraction, their cover was blown and Hunter Cabot had been shot. Zack and the rest of the team had made it back to the Zodiac boat with the hostage before they'd realized Hunter was missing.

Zack had reported in and had been given the order to cut Hunter loose and get the hell out of Dodge. Just remembering the easy dismissal of a SEAL's life made him furious all over again. Zack's hand tightened around his beer. No way in hell would he agree to leaving one of his team behind. So he'd disregarded orders, left the team to guard the hostage and went back in himself to drag Hunter's ass out.

Now Hunter was recovering in the hospital, surrounded by gorgeous nurses and Zack had been sentenced to serve as nursemaid to a geek.

Yeah, life was fair.

"What kind of fish, you think?"

"Huh?" Frowning, Zack looked at Danny.

"I mean," his friend said, "maybe its something interesting like sharks. Back home I saw a shark once, big enough to—"

"Please." Zack held up a hand and winced. "No Hawaiian folk tales today, okay?"

Nothing Danny liked better than telling tall tales about the beauty of Hawaii, the big waves, the gorgeous women and just how many of those women were nuts about Danny Akiona. Zack wasn't in the mood.

Danny grinned. "Fine. When do you go see the fish woman?"

"I'm a free man until tomorrow morning, 0800."

"Hell, brudda," Danny used the island slang for "brother," and his voice was almost musical as he added, "that leaves us all of tonight."

Zack smiled, feeling a little better. Eight o'clock was hours away yet. No point in acting like he was in prison until the cell door actually slammed shut. "You're right."

"Damn straight." Danny signaled the waitress for another round of drinks, then looked at Zack. "I say we find us a couple of ladies and then pack in a whole month's worth of R and R into one night. If it's your last, let's make it count, brudda."

One night. Hell, they'd done it before. He and Danny had torn up towns and welcomed the dawn in too many countries to count. No reason why he couldn't have a big blowout the night before starting a new assignment.

Whatever Kimberly Danforth—God, what a snooty name—was like, the fish geek wouldn't have to be faced until tomorrow. And as any SEAL knew, you lived life one moment at a time, 'cause you never knew if you'd get another.

"I've said it before, I'll say it again," Zack said, ordering himself to relax and enjoy the rest of the night. "Hula," he said, using Danny's team nickname, "I like your style."

Kim Danforth glared at the telephone receiver in her hand and then slapped it back against her ear. Frustration bubbled inside her, blending with the blossoming sense that she was losing this battle. "Dad, this is ridiculous. I don't want a guard dog and I certainly don't *need* one."

Abraham Danforth's voice, fluid, strong and commanding, came across the line. "Kimberly, do this for me. These threats are not to be ignored."

Fear for her father's safety took the edge off her frustration and she winced. "Dad, first of all, it's only one threat and it was made against *you,* not me."

There was a long pause and she heard him inhale slowly, deeply. She counted to ten, knowing he was doing the same. Always careful about what he said, Abraham prided himself on his self-control. Even around the family dinner table, he'd always weighed every word, thinking carefully before speaking. Which was only one of the reasons why he made such an excellent senatorial candidate.

"Kimberly, whoever is behind this would know that the surest way to hurt me would be to hurt my family."

Kim sighed. Her father hadn't always been the most involved, caring parent. A man of business, he'd spent most of his energies growing the Danforth bank balances rather than spending time with his five kids. But he loved his children, and she knew he worried most about her, his youngest child and only daughter.

She also knew that a part of her father was using this situation as an attempt to be the kind of father he wished he'd been when she was growing up. The stalker sending threatening e-mail messages to Abraham hadn't threatened his family. Kim knew perfectly well that she wasn't in any real danger— which made the idea of having a bodyguard that much harder to accept. But she couldn't bring herself to turn her father down and give him one more thing to worry about.

Besides, her dad's younger brother, her uncle Harold, had asked her to go along with her father's request. Uncle Harold had said the entire family would be relieved if she was safe.

"Give the old man a break, will you?" he asked.

She smiled and shook her head. There was simply no way out of this. Between her father and her uncle, she was outnumbered and she knew it. Harold Danforth had been a substitute father to her and her brothers. Without the responsibilities of running the Danforth business interests, he'd had more time to give to both his own children and Abraham's.

"Fine," she said. "He can protect me. But he's not living here."

"There's room." Abraham's voice became abrupt as if now that he'd won the argument, he was ready to move on. "Just put him up in your spare room."

"Dad, I'm not letting a stranger stay in my house."

"He's not a stranger. He's the son of—"

"Your old navy buddy, I know," she said interrupting him before she heard the old war stories again. The only war she was interested in at the moment was the personal war for her own independence.

"Zack should be there any minute," her father was saying. "I expect you to cooperate."

"Dad—"

"Have to run now."

The dial tone ringing in her ear kept her from arguing further. "Nice chatting with you, Dad," she said tightly, wishing that just once, she could have gotten in the last word.

When the doorbell rang a few minutes later, Kim was still primed for battle.

She opened the door to a grim-faced man in dark glasses. He seemed to take up a lot of space on her small, flower-filled front porch. Was this Navy SEAL supposed to be her protector? Weren't military men a little better groomed? "Yes?"

The man frowned and reached up to rub his forehead. "Do you have to shout?" His voice sounded creaky, careful.

"I wasn't shouting."

"You're *still* shouting," he told her and reluctantly took off his sunglasses, wincing at the brightness of the day. "Man, morning sucks."

Kim stared up at him. *Way* up. A couple of inches over six feet tall, the man was broad in the shoulders, had a narrow waist and legs long enough for two men. His reddish brown hair was cut militarily high and tight. His ancient jeans were threadbare at the knee and faded. The collar of his dark red shirt was twisted, one side up, the other tucked beneath the neck of the shirt. He also wore a dark blue sweatshirt that looked as worn as his jeans. His narrowed eyes were a mixture of blue and green—and the red streaks surrounding the irises told her he'd had a late night.

This couldn't be the man her father was sending, she told herself. Zack Sheridan was a Navy SEAL—not a man she'd expect to show up with a hangover and two days' worth of stubble on his square jaws.

She wished suddenly for a steel security screen door.

"What do you want?"

"Loaded question," he said, his voice a low rumble that seemed to vibrate right through her without even trying. "What I want," he said, "is aspirin, a dark room...and to be anywhere but here."

"Charming," she said, clutching the door in a tight grip, ready to slam it home and lock it. "Why don't you go get those things? Start with the last one and go away."

She swung the door closed, but he shoved one sneaker-clad foot between the door and the jamb.

Kim narrowed her eyes on him and ignored the curl of fear in the pit of her stomach. Naturally, she didn't let him know it. "Move that foot mister, or I'll break it."

"Let's start over," he said, not moving the foot an inch.

"Let's not." She pushed the door harder.

His mouth tightened. "That hurts, you know."

"That's sort of the point."

He sighed. "You Kimberly Danforth?"

"Is that supposed to ensure my trust? You knowing my name?" She put her whole weight behind the door now and thought she felt it budge.

He slapped one hand on the door and pushed back. With very little effort, he managed to shove the door open a crack farther.

"Hey. Let go of my door."

"I'm Zack Sheridan."

"Good for you."

"Your father sent me."

She released her hold on the door and his heavy hand pushed it wide open until it swung back and slammed into the wall behind it.

"Damn, you're loud," he muttered, reaching one hand to his forehead again as if trying to hold his skull together.

Kim was rethinking this whole proposition. The man was obviously hungover, not exactly inspiring a lot of trust. He looked more like a pirate than a navy SEAL. Danger emanated from him, reached out toward her, and gave her nerves a little shake.

If there was a trickle of pure female appreciation mixed in with the trepidation rolling through her stomach, she chose to ignore it.

Sure, she'd agreed to her father's request. But she had a feeling that Abraham Danforth wouldn't be so in favor of Zack staying with his little girl if he could get a good look at the man.

So she went with her instincts.

"I don't want you here," Kim said, lifting her chin and meeting his gaze squarely. "I don't need you here, either, despite what my father thinks."

"Lady, I just take orders."

"A centuries-old claim of innocence."

"Huh?" Those blue-green eyes of his narrowed.

"Look." She pulled her glasses off the collar of her V-necked blue T-shirt and put them on. She only used the glasses for reading, but she'd found out long ago that wearing them gave her a little distance. "I don't need your help, so why don't you just go?"

"Wish I could," he said and stepped into her house, practically sighing at the cool shade of the room.

"Well, please. Come in," she said dryly.

He glanced around the room as if she hadn't spoken and Kim followed his gaze, looking at her home through a stranger's eyes.

The small, two-bedroom cottage was more than a hundred years old, with all the charm and foibles of an antique. The plumbing wasn't the greatest, but there were built-in bookshelves and a built-in china hutch in the kitchen. There were niches cut into the walls for vases of flowers, but the bathroom was pitifully small. The yard was no bigger than a postage stamp, but the tree in the front yard was eighty years old and gave much-needed shade in summer.

The living room was, like the rest of the place, tiny. But the soft blue walls looked like a cloudless summer sky. A blue-and-white plaid sofa sat in front of a miniature tiled hearth and brightly colored rag rugs dotted the glistening wood floor. On the walls, she'd hung framed photos from her travels and a couple of paintings done by a marine artist. It was home. It was all hers. And she didn't want to share it.

Not even temporarily.

"Nice place," he said.

"Thank you. Now, if you don't mind—"

"Lady…" He folded his arms across his pretty impressive chest and stared down at her through bloodshot eyes. "Whether you like it or not, we're in this together."

The room suddenly felt a lot smaller and the air a little warmer. "I don't like it."

"If you think my idea of a vacation is riding herd on a fish geek—"

"Excuse me?" Kim straightened up to her less-than-impressive five feet seven inches and tried to look down her nose at him. Not easy to do when she had to tilt her head back all the way to meet his gaze. "I happen to be a Doctor of Marine Biology."

"Yeah? So?"

"So I prefer that term to *fish geek*."

"Who wouldn't?" He chuckled, then the sound trailed off as he caught her irritation. "Fine. *Doctor* Danforth…"

She nodded.

"Climb down off your high dolphin because for the next little while, you and me are gonna be best friends."

Something hot and sharp and really annoying blasted through her. "I don't—"

He cocked his head and gave her a patient smile he probably reserved for small children and half-wits.

"I'm calling my father." A bluff, but it was all she had.

He nodded. "Give him my best."

Kim's small flicker of irritation burst like a Fourth of July firecracker. No way was she going to be able to have this man living in her home for thirty days. "I'll call your commanding officer to complain."

Zack plopped down onto one of her chairs, sighed and stretched out his long legs in front of him like a man settling in and getting comfortable. "He'll be happy to know I reported to duty on time."

Kim was losing control. She felt it slipping from her fingers like the string of a helium balloon on a windy day. Of course his commanding officer wouldn't listen to her. Her father had already seen to that.

"I'll call the police. They'll arrest you."

For one brief moment, hope lit up his eyes. "You think?" Then he shook his head. "Nah. Forget it, darlin'."

She stiffened. "Don't call me darlin'."

He slipped his sunglasses on, rested his head on the chair back and sighed. "No darlin'. Got it."

"This isn't going to work out," Kim said tightly.

Tipping his shades down a fraction of an inch, he gave her a warm look and a smile that sent something completely unexpected scuttling through her. ''Baby, I'm a SEAL. I can make anything work.''

Two

Zack watched her stalk around the small room, phone in hand, muttering a string of complaints to whoever was unfortunate enough to be on the other end of the line.

She was hopping mad.

And damn, she looked good.

He smiled to himself. Slitting his eyes as a defense against the morning sunlight flooding the room, he admired the woman who was somehow more than he'd expected. Who would have thought a fish geek would be so nicely put together?

Her sky-blue, V-necked shirt clung to her small, high breasts like a lover's hands. Her long legs were hidden from him in a pair of khaki-colored drawstring pants that dipped beneath her belly button, giving him a tantalizing glimpse of smooth, tanned skin. Her long, straight, midnight-black hair was gathered into a ponytail that swung in a wide arc across her back as she marched furiously around the room.

"I don't care if he's in a meeting," she said, louder now. "I want to speak to my father, *now*." A pause, then, "Fine. I'll hold."

"Won't work," Zack muttered and she flipped him a quick look.

"What won't?"

"Getting rid of me." When her frown deepened and her big, grass-green eyes narrowed on him, Zack almost chuckled. Damn, she got prettier the madder she got. And he was just ornery enough to enjoy the show. "I tried to get out of this, but no way."

"You tried?"

Another dry chuckle sounded from his throat. "You think this is my idea of a good time?"

Thoughtful, she cupped one hand over the mouth of the phone. "Why'd you agree to it?"

"Long story." He folded his hands atop his abdomen and drummed his fingers. Zack wasn't going to get into the whole sad tale about his too-many-to-count futile stands against authority. It was none of her business and besides, he didn't want to think about it. "Let's just say it beat the hell out of the alternative."

"Must have been some alternative."

"Trust me."

"That's the point here," she said. "I don't."

"Bottom line," Zack said, fatigue dragging at him, "I go against this order, and I kiss my commission goodbye. I'm not willing to do that."

"Fine." Clearly coming to a decision, she hung up the phone then turned to face him. Folding her arms beneath her breasts, she hitched one nicely rounded hip higher than the other and tapped her bare toes against the rag rug. "If this is going to work, I think we should come up with some ground rules."

"Yeah?" Zack smiled. Couldn't help it. Her small, wire-framed glasses glinted in the sunlight and her full lips thinned into what she probably considered a firm line. Black eyebrows were arched high on her forehead and her glasses slipped a bit down her small, straight nose. Not exactly the intimidating picture she was no doubt hoping for.

"Shoot."

"Don't tempt me."

He snorted a laugh. "Damned if I couldn't start to like you."

"Why, my little heart's just fluttering."

He grinned.

She almost smiled back and Zack felt a solid but invisible punch in his midsection. Damn, the fish geek had some secret weapons other than that trim, compact body.

"Okay, here's my suggestion," she said.

Zack waited.

"I'll put up with you and you can fulfill your orders to protect me during the day..."

"And?"

"And at night, you'll go away."

"Tempting, but no deal."

She threw both hands up and let them slap against her thighs. "Why not?"

"Because," he said, pushing himself up from the chair that was way too comfortable for a man as sleep-deprived as he was. "My orders say I stick to you like a stamp on a letter for the next month. That's what I'm gonna do."

"It's not necessary."

"And if you were an admiral," Zack told her, "I'd take your word for it."

She practically vibrated with impatience. "Surely you can see this house is too small for two people."

"It's a little...cozy." He'd dug foxholes with more maneuvering room.

"It's not even a real two-bedroom. It's a one-bedroom house that somebody broke up into two rooms with a few two-by-fours and a couple of sheets of plywood.''

"Your point?"

"There's no room for you."

"The couch'll do me."

"It won't do for me."

"You don't get a vote."

"How do I not get a vote?'' she echoed and he could actually see the fury mounting in her eyes. "This is my house."

"And I'm your guest."

She fumed silently for a long minute and Zack wondered if she was planning to make a break for it. But he didn't think so. She seemed too stubborn for a surrender.

He was right.

"I don't take orders well."

He smiled. "Me, neither. We'll probably make a good team."

"I doubt it."

Zack studied her for a long minute, until he had the satisfaction of seeing her shift uncomfortably. He was willing to make nice—but he'd be damned if he'd be stonewalled by some scientist.

"Doctor Danforth, I don't want to be here any more than you want me to be here."

"Then—"

"It doesn't change the fact that I am here. And here I stay until my superior orders me to get out."

* * *

Kim tiptoed through the dark house, grateful that she'd had her floorboards treated six months before. They didn't squeak anymore, so her progress through the tiny house was absolutely silent.

Careful not to breathe too heavily, she clutched her house keys tightly in one fist so they wouldn't rattle together. A sly smile curved her mouth and she hugged her deception to her. It was almost fun, she thought. Putting one over on the mighty SEAL who'd been assigned to watch her every move.

She hadn't had fun in a very long time, and if it wasn't necessary to be quiet, she might have given in to the urge to chuckle. After all, to anyone looking in through a window, she would have appeared ridiculous. Sneaking through her own house like a burglar.

Inching past the door leading to the tiny second bedroom she used as an office—and for now, a makeshift guest room for the invader—her heart slowed to a more reasonable beat. As she stepped quietly around the hall corner leading to the living room, it occurred to her that she'd never sneaked before in her life.

Girls at her private high school used to talk about slipping out of their houses to meet boys. And then having to slip back in before dawn to avoid both parents and servants. But Kim had never done it herself. She'd always been the "good" one. The obedient one. The respectful one.

The boring one, she thought now.

Shaking her head, she gritted her teeth and pushed those old memories to the back of her mind. No point in reliving them now, for heaven's sake. Besides, Johnny-come-lately or not, she was finally doing a little sneaking. Even if it was out of her own house.

Moonlight slid through the white curtains at the windows and lay like God's nightlight over the room. Eyes accustomed to the dim lighting and so familiar with her own house she could have walked through it blindfolded, Kim headed for the front door. Carefully, she turned the deadbolt until it snapped clear with an audible click.

She winced at the sound and held her breath, waiting.

When she didn't hear anything, she smiled to herself again and closed her fingers over the cold brass knob. Slowly, she turned it and the soft sigh of the door coming away from the jamb sounded like a shriek to her anxious ears. But again, there was no sound from her guard dog. Another step or two and she'd be clear. She could go about her nightly routine without worrying about being followed. Without having to put up with a man she didn't want or need in her life.

Kim eased through the doorway, pushed the

screen door open, then stepped onto the porch. She turned around and relocked the deadbolt with a nearly silent *snick* of sound. After all, she didn't want to leave the guard dog unprotected.

Pleased with herself, she eased the screen door closed, turned around—and crashed into a broad, hard chest.

Her screech, set at a level only dogs should have been able to hear, rattled Zack's brain and, he was pretty sure, made his ears bleed. Before he could check, though, she recovered.

Lifting her right leg, she slammed her heel down onto his instep. While the dazzling pain of that move was still fresh, she whirled and rammed her elbow into his midsection. Surprise, added to the blow, had all of his air leaving him in a rush.

Stunned, Zack tried to figure out how a fish geek had gotten the drop on him.

But as she moved again, lightning fast, his own survival instincts kicked in—just in time to save his esophagus from being speared by her rigid fingers.

Zack grabbed her wrist and held on. ''Damn it, Doc, it's me.''

She fought against his grasp, tugging and pulling until slowly, she eased off and he knew his words had gotten through. She stared up at him, and he saw her pulse pounding raggedly at the base of her neck. Breath rushed in and out of her lungs and her wide green eyes looked huge in the moonlight.

"You?" One word, strangled out from a throat obviously still tight with fear.

"Yeah, so cool your jets, huh?"

"Cool my..." She sucked in air, then drew her free hand back and jammed her closed fist into his abdomen.

This time though, he'd been ready for the attack. Tensing his muscles, he felt her blow glance off his body like a rock off the still surface of a lake.

"Hit me again," he muttered as he grabbed her other wrist, "and I just might hit you back, darlin'."

"Don't call me darlin'."

"Don't hit me."

She kicked him.

He winced. Shouldn't have challenged her, he thought wearily. "Fine," he admitted. "So I won't hit you back." Still holding on to her, he eased back far enough that kicking him would take some real effort. "But I *will* tie you to a chair."

She ignored that and wriggled in his grip like a worm trying to escape the hook.

"What the hell do you think you're doing?" she said, her words coming fast and furious. Fear still stained her voice and smeared the air between them. "You scared me to death."

"I didn't mean to. I only meant to stop you."

"Well, you did both. Happy now?"

He grinned down at her. Scared or not, she'd done all right. Way better than he'd expected. And standing here in the dark, watching her breasts rise and fall with her rapid breathing, was giving him a few ideas about seeing if other things about the fish geek would be better than he'd expected, too.

"Fight pretty good for a corpse," he said.

She blew out a breath. "That's not funny."

"Not a lot of laughs from where I'm standing, either," he said, releasing one of her wrists to rub one palm over his stomach.

She caught the action. "Did I hurt you?"

Let's see, he thought. A one-hundred-twenty-pound female throws a lucky punch and actually hurts him? Not a chance. But damn, she looked so hopeful, he heard himself say, "Yeah."

"Good." She yanked her other hand free and rubbed at her wrist long enough to make Zack worry that he'd hurt *her*.

"You okay?"

"I'm fine." She stepped a wide path around him, then turned her head back to level a long look at him. "What I want to know is what are you doing out here?"

"Waiting for you."

Her eyes narrowed on him.

"You heard me?"

He'd been awake and alert from the moment she

started moving around in her room. Her attempt at "stealthy" wasn't all that great. Of course, maybe it would have worked on some regular guy who didn't always have one ear cocked and ready for the sound of a threat coming out of nowhere.

For Zack though, waking from a dead sleep to red-alert status was nothing new. He'd been trained to sleep with one eye open. And that ability had saved his ass on more than one occasion. Once he'd gotten used to the night sounds of her house, her neighborhood, the small, subtle sounds coming from her room had told him she was on the move.

He hadn't figured her for the type to try an escape in the dead of night. He'd looked at her wire-rimmed glasses and trim, tight figure and the stacks of books she surrounded herself with and told himself she'd be no trouble at all.

Which only went to prove that it was possible to surprise a SEAL.

"Yeah, I heard you." No point in telling her that he'd slipped out the window in his room, scooted around the edge of the house and waited on the front porch while she made her escape. The evidence was here in front of her. Besides, if he told her what not to do, she'd only use it against him at another time.

He was beginning to see that riding herd on Kim Danforth wasn't going to be the walk in the park that he'd expected.

"You must have ears like a bat," she muttered and went down the front steps without another look at him.

"I heard that well enough." He was just a step behind her. Far enough back not to crowd her, but close enough that he got a real good view of her excellent behind. She wore black jeans and a black jacket over a black sweatshirt. Her midnight-colored hair was coiled into a tight knot at the back of her neck.

Zack's night vision was good enough to notice just how well those jeans fit her. And his imagination was good enough to picture everything that was hidden beneath the too-bulky jacket and sweatshirt.

"Any particular reason you're dressed like a burglar?" he asked conversationally as he kept just a step or two behind her.

"You've discovered my secret life," she said, sarcasm dripping from every word. "I'm a cat burglar."

He grinned and shook his head. "Then you can answer a question for me. I've always wondered why somebody would go to all the trouble to break into a house just to steal a cat."

She stopped, looked back at him and smirked. "I had no idea SEALs were such comedians."

"See? Learn something new every day."

"Then since your lesson plan is concluded, go away."

"Nope." Zack's long legs closed the distance between them quickly and he fell into step beside her. "Where you go, I go."

"I don't want you."

"I don't care."

She stopped under a streetlight and glared up at him. And damned if Zack wasn't starting to like the look of those green eyes firing sparks at him.

"You don't seem to understand," she said and her voice adopted the standard professor's this-is-a-lecture-pay-close-attention tone that used to put him to sleep at the Naval Academy. "I don't need you here. I don't want you here."

Zack stared down into those eyes and then let his gaze move over her features. Her cool, creamy skin gleamed like porcelain in the pale wash of the streetlight. She looked a damn sight better than he'd expected a scientist to look. And she was more stubborn than he'd been prepared for. Not to mention she had a real nasty, sharp-edged tongue on her when her temper was on the boil. She was sneaky, underhanded and a dirty fighter.

Add all of that to great legs, an excellent behind and a pair of small, high breasts that he was itching to cup, and you had a hell of a package.

"Doc," he said when he could tell by the tightening of her lips that she was on the edge of temper again, "you don't have a say in this."

"But—"

"Now." He cut her off, dropped one arm around her shoulders and started walking in the direction she'd been headed a minute or so before. "We can stand here and argue, or we can keep walking and argue as we go. What'll it be?"

She pushed his arm off her shoulders. "I can walk and talk at the same time. You sure you're up to the challenge?"

"Damned if I'm not getting real fond of you, darlin'."

Three

Kim completely ignored the still-sizzling sensation of heat that was rocketing through her body. She'd pushed his arm off almost instantly, and yet, despite the cold night air, her skin hummed and her blood was bubbling in her veins.

She couldn't even remember the last time a man had had that sort of effect on her. In fact, she was pretty sure it had never happened before.

This was probably not a good sign.

He walked beside her, his long, jeans-clad legs moving in time with hers. She felt him watching her from the corner of his eye and in response, she kept her own gaze locked straight ahead. She wouldn't let him know that he was getting to her.

"So where're we going?" he asked.

"I'm going to the riverfront. I have no idea where you're going."

"Wherever you go, sweetheart. Just consider me your shadow."

She glanced at him, then away again. "Shadows are quiet."

"I can do quiet, but what's the point?" He shrugged and she caught the movement from the corner of her eye. "We're stuck together, peaches. So we may as well be friendly."

Friendly? He wasn't her friend. Kim didn't have many of those and the ones she did have weren't six foot tall, gorgeous, greeny-blue-eyed guard dogs. And they certainly didn't set her blood boiling with a simple touch. In fact, she didn't have any male friends. Strange, now that she thought about it, but true. She'd never been the kind of woman men paid attention to.

She'd been the studious one. The one with straight As. The one who, when she was at college, spent her Friday nights at the library instead of attending frat parties. Maybe it was having grown up with four older brothers, she thought.

They'd been great, but with the Danforth brothers standing between her and boys, there hadn't been many willing to risk running the gauntlet. As a teenager, she'd hoped for a boyfriend, but had finally settled for the Principal's

Honor Roll. When that situation continued through college, she'd slipped into the rut she found herself in now. No real life. Just her job. She was thankful it was one she loved...but that didn't change the whole lack-of-a-life thing.

But she was better off than some of the women she knew. Working on their third or fourth husbands, fighting custody battles and going to spas to maintain the figures they hoped would win them another trip down the aisle.

She didn't envy them the lawyers and hard feelings and bitter divorce settlements. Kim was still enough of a closet romantic to believe that marriage should last forever. Which probably explained why she was still single.

"Look," she said, coming at the current problem as she did everything else in her world, with calm logic. "I have things to do. I don't need an escort or a guard. I don't want your company and I'm not your friend. So why don't you go back to the house and wait for me?"

"Does that usually work?"

"What?"

"That quiet, teacher-to-student voice," he said, one corner of his mouth tilting into a smile that nearly curled Kim's toes. "Do the men you date actually go for that? Just roll over and do what you want?"

"I don't—"

"Know?"

"Date," she corrected.

"Never?"

Kim stopped and stared up at him. They were in between streetlights, so his face was mostly in shadows. But why did she know he was smiling again?

"That really isn't any of your business."

"Call it curiosity."

"Call it intrusive."

"Big word."

"Need a dictionary?"

He laughed and the deep, rolling sound of it washed over her. Stunned, Kim just looked at him. Normally her sarcasm put people off. Or scared them off. Apparently, Zack Sheridan was different.

But she'd known that right from the start, hadn't she?

"You've got a hell of a mouth on you."

She blew out a breath. "I tend to say whatever I happen to be thinking at the time."

He shook his head. "I wasn't talking about what you said. I was talking about your mouth."

Her breath lodged in her throat. "What?"

He reached out and rubbed his thumb over her bottom lip. "Wide smile, great snarl and lush, full lips."

She pulled her head back. Too late to stop the jolt of electricity ricocheting around her blood stream, but quick enough to keep her from asking him to touch her some more.

Oh, wow. Where had that come from?

Too much alone time, Kim thought. Just way too much. She should get out more. Join a bowling league. Take line-dancing lessons. *Something.* Then she wouldn't be bowled over by a man who probably had a string of women trailing in his wake.

That image straightened her up.

"I really have to go," she said and started walking again.

Wind off the river brushed past her, the cold damp of it sliding into her bones and wiping away the lingering heat Zack's touch had ignited. Good. That was good.

The houses they passed were dark but for the occasional glimpses of lamplight pooling behind curtains. Ordinarily, on her late-night walks, she indulged herself with wondering what was going on behind those curtains. What kind of people lived in the well-tended old homes. Were they laughing, crying? Wondering how to pay the bills or planning a vacation?

She told herself she didn't mind always being on the outside looking in, but once in a while, when she heard a baby's cry or a child's laughter, she would wish that there was someone at home waiting for her. Someone she could talk to, turn to in the night. Someone to worry about. Someone to love.

Tonight, someone *was* with her. For all the wrong reasons. Indulging in flights of fancy was impossible, too. How could she wonder about strangers when she had her very own personal stranger walking right beside her, ruining her routine?

"Do this often?" he asked.

"Hmm?"

"Stroll around in the dead of night all by yourself?"

She slid him a glance. "I'm a big girl."

"I noticed," he pointed out, then let his gaze drift across the darkened street. "Most other red-blooded guys would notice, too."

That had never really been her problem, but he didn't have to know that. "Darn. I forgot my stick."

"What stick?"

"The one I use to beat all the men off me."

"That's real cute, honey. But the point is, a woman walking alone at night is looking for trouble."

"Excuse me?" Kim stopped again, this time directly under a streetlight, with a three storied, gingerbread covered Victorian beauty behind her. Tipping her head back, she told herself to pay no attention to the way the light and shadow fell on his features, making him look both unreasonably attractive and dangerous. "Because I'm taking a walk at night it would be my fault if I get attacked?"

"Not your fault, but you do present a window of opportunity."

"Right. Well, I can take care of myself."

"I remember." He rubbed one hand over his stomach again.

"Oh, please. I didn't hurt you."

"True. Surprised me, though."

"I grew up with four brothers. You learn a thing or two."

"They taught you that instep move?"

"Among other things." She let her gaze slip down to his groin briefly.

He grinned. "Now that would hurt."

"Supposed to."

He gave her an approving nod. "Your brothers were thorough."

Not to mention the self-defense courses she'd taken. But Kim didn't think he needed to know that. She wasn't an idiot. She knew how important it was for a woman to be able to protect herself. Especially a woman who up until today had lived alone.

"I told you, I don't need a bodyguard."

"Uh-huh. But I'm willing to bet a Navy SEAL

knows a few more things about defense than you do.''

Yes, but could a Navy SEAL tell her how to protect herself against a Navy SEAL? That was the real question. And one she didn't think she could ask Zack.

"Fine." She threw up her hands in surrender. "Let's just go, all right?"

"We're making progress," he said, falling into step beside her again. "At least you admit you're not going to shake me."

"For now." But she had hopes, Kim told herself. In the morning, she'd call her father again. Try to talk to him about this rationally, calmly. And if that didn't work, she'd call Uncle Harold and whine. And if that didn't work...well, a person could only have so many plans at once.

She walked along the river's edge, moonlight glinting off the darkness of her hair and the creamy coolness of her skin. She seemed to notice everything—from the trash she picked up as she walked, to the stray cat hiding in the oat grass near the water's edge.

She ignored him for the most part and that was all right with him. He didn't need to get to know her. She was just an assignment and after thirty days, he'd be moving on. But he couldn't help noticing things about her. Hell, he was a trained observer.

Her hands were small, fine-boned and delicate looking. Her legs were long and looked damn good in those dark jeans. Her sneakers were battered and her jacket was new, but had two missing buttons and a torn pocket. She was a contrast, he thought. A woman who came from more money than he'd likely see in a lifetime, but who spent her nights picking up litter and wandering a riverbank alone.

Why wasn't she out on a date with some good-looking, fast-talking guy with a bank balance higher than his IQ? Why wasn't she at a party in some sleek black dress with diamonds at her throat?

Why did he care?

He didn't.

Zack shoved his hands into his jeans pockets and kept a step or two behind her. A cold, damp wind rustled in off the water and tugged at her hair, teasing a few long strands free of the knot at the nape of her neck to swirl about her face. She stared out at the river as if looking well beyond the dark water into the distance. When she took a deep breath and blew it out, he nearly felt her distraction.

Hell, he sympathized. He didn't like anyone hanging around cramping his free time, either— when he had some. But sometimes, life just smacked you in the face and you had to deal with it.

His sharp gaze moved across the area for the hundredth time in the last half hour. He was a man used to trouble and he liked to be ready and waiting when it came knocking.

But this small slice of Savannah was quiet and nearly deserted. One or two couples wandered along the river walk, hand in hand, stopping now and then for a kiss that made Zack think wistfully about things other than baby-sitting a beautiful nerd. But then the couples moved on and it was just the two of them in the darkness.

Wrought-iron grillwork lined the river walk, with low-lying shrubs and now-dormant flowering plants crowded close together at the base of the trees. In another month or two, the flowers would be blooming and the night air would already be starting to steam up in anticipation of summer. Moonlight glittered on the surface of the river, and the sound of the water rushing past was almost like a whisper in a quiet room.

Kim swiveled her head, looking first up the river and then down again.

Zack moved in closer.

"Are you looking for something?"

"No."

"So why come down here?"

She turned her face to his. She looked cool and

remote and somehow incredibly appealing. "I like the water."

It made sense. Why be a fish geek if you preferred dry land?

"Me, too," he said and briefly studied the surface of the dark, swiftly moving river. "Give me an ocean and I'm a happy man."

"Makes sense for a Navy SEAL."

He glanced back at her. "Or a marine biologist. So what's a woman who studies ocean life doing down at a river in the middle of the night?"

She turned her face back toward the water and Zack caught the far-off look in her eyes. As if she was, at least mentally, a long way from Savannah.

"The ocean's eighteen miles away. I don't like driving at night."

"You don't mind walking for miles."

She smiled. Just a slight lift of her lips and it was gone again but for that one instant, Zack felt the slam of that smile hit him low and hard. He knew the signs of attraction. He just hadn't expected to feel them for a fish geek.

"Walking's different." She shrugged. "Relaxing. Driving, I'd be all tense and gripping the steering wheel."

"You do this often?"

"Every night."

"A routine?"

She looked at him again. "I guess. Why?"

He shrugged, but the movement belied his suddenly more alert status. "Routines can be dangerous. Anyone watching you would know in a couple of days of surveillance that he could find you here. Alone. At night."

Her shoulders hunched and she stuffed her hands into her coat pockets and drew the fabric tight across her middle. "Nobody's watching me."

"Can't be sure."

"I'd know."

"So you're a psychic fish doctor?"

"I'm not a fish doctor."

"But you are psychic?"

"No. Are you always this annoying?"

"Yes. So you don't know if somebody's watching you."

She paused, her gaze narrowed on the river and her mouth worked as if she wanted to argue with him. Eventually though, she sighed. "I guess not."

He admired her independence and her willingness to fight to protect her own space and way of life. But damned if he didn't also admire her for being willing to admit when she was wrong. In his experience, not many people were big enough to handle that. "Wasn't so hard, was it?"

"What?"

Her gaze was turned up to him again and he noticed that even in the dark, her eyes were a clear and startling green. Made a man wish he could just let himself fall into their depths and sink. That thought brought Zack up short. "Admitting you might need help."

"I didn't actually admit that," she corrected primly. "What I said was, I don't know if someone's watching me. But I'm betting, no."

"Willing to bet your life on that?"

"You're here, aren't you?"

"So I am."

"Look," she said, "my father's worried, that's why I'm letting you stay. There is no danger to me."

"Not as long as I'm here," he said, one corner of his mouth tilting up in a crooked smile.

She frowned. "I like taking care of myself."

"Me, too," he admitted and reached out to tug the collar of her jacket up higher around her neck. The backs of his fingers brushed along her throat and she shivered. Before that shiver could slide into him, Zack let her go again and stuffed his hands into his pockets. "We have something in common."

"Maybe," she conceded.

"Maybe'll do for a start." He took a step back, not sure why exactly, just knowing that a little distance wouldn't be a bad thing. But as he looked into her eyes, he felt himself wanting to look even deeper. Over the next thirty days, he was probably going to require a hell of a lot more distance than a couple of feet.

Four

The next day, their first battle was fought over breakfast.

Early-morning sunlight streamed in through the kitchen window, lying across the blue-and-gray linoleum, the blue granite counter and then glinting off the sparkling, stainless-steel refrigerator. A trio of small clay pots lined the windowsill and boasted tiny herb seedlings. Through that same window came the sounds of birds singing, kids laughing and, from a distance, a lawnmower growling.

Life in the neighborhood was ordinary, normal. Life in Kim's house was anything but.

Bent over double, head in the refrigerator, Zack asked, "Where's the bacon?"

"There isn't any." Kim stirred honey into her herbal tea, then lifted it for a sip.

"Eggs?" His voice was muffled, hopeful.

"Nope," she said, then offered, "There's a carton of egg substitute on the top shelf."

He straightened up, still holding the fridge door open and looked at her, clearly appalled. "Does that come complete with taste substitute?"

She ignored that. "I have some whole wheat bagels and low-fat cream cheese."

He shuddered and closed the refrigerator. "That's what you eat?"

"It's healthy."

"So's grazing in a field," he pointed out. "And just about as tasty."

She smiled. If he was less than comfortable at her place, maybe he'd leave. "You're cranky in the mornings, aren't you?"

He reached up and pushed both hands along the sides of his skull, skimming his palms over his short, neat hair. Kim's gaze drifted briefly to his broad chest hidden beneath a clean white T-shirt. Even through the fabric, she could see the play of his muscles, shifting, flexing.

Heat rushed through her, so she took another sip of tea in an attempt to cool herself down. Oh, yeah. That made sense.

When Zack's hands dropped to his sides again, he gave her a disgusted look before shifting his gaze. He took in the kitchen, with her tidy countertop, the toaster, the blender and the microwave. Finally, he shifted that steady gaze to her. "Where's the coffee pot?"

"I don't have one. I don't drink coffee."

His eyes bugged out. "No coffee?"

"There's tea."

He considered that for a minute or two. "Is it caffeinated?"

"No. Herbal."

"Good God, woman," he muttered, crossing the tiny, galley-style kitchen to sit at the small, round table opposite her. "How can you get going in the morning without a shot of caffeine?"

"Wake up, get up, get dressed and go."

"That's not human."

"Jolting your system with caffeine is crazy."

"Bet you don't drink beer, either, do you?"

"For breakfast?" She smiled.

He shook his head, scowled darkly and leaned back in his chair, folding his arms over his chest. "You're a hard woman."

Not at the moment, she thought as she felt his gaze lock on her. In fact, everything inside her was soft and squishy and sort of like a marshmallow toasted over an open fire.

Kim watched him and wondered how she was going to get through the next month. The house was too small. Too confined. And with Zack Sheridan in residence, it felt downright Lilliputian. He not only took up a lot of room—being as big as he was—but there were the constant reminders of his presence.

For instance, having to stand in the hall and listen to him shower.

Fine, she could have gone into the living room where the rush of water would have been more subtle. But once her mind had drawn the image of Zack, naked, under a stream of hot water, steam rising all around him, she'd been caught. Mesmerized by her own imagination.

Which was really ridiculous.

He wasn't even her type.

But then, she didn't have a type, did she?

Most men walked right past her as if she weren't there. Or, if they did stop to talk to her, it only meant that they'd discovered her last name was Danforth. They never looked at her and saw Kim. They took one look and saw a bank account.

Frowning, she stopped that train of thought and lifted her tea for another sip. Over the rim of the fragile china cup, she watched the man now drumming his fingers on the table top.

He looked like a chained tiger. Energy coursed around him in an aura that was practically vibrating with the need to move.

"Okay, I'm willing to put up with a lot. But I'm gonna need coffee in the mornings."

"There's a D & D coffee bar on the next block."

"Thank God." Then he looked at her thoughtfully. "D & D. Doesn't your family own those places?"

Here it comes, she thought and she willed away the tiny twinge of disappointment. The speculation. The mental addition all men did when they tried to work out just how much she might be worth. She'd be able to see it in his eyes, she knew. He'd wonder, consider and try to decide if the money was worth hitting on her.

A long moment ticked past.

Her fingers tightened on her teacup.

"You own coffee bars and don't drink the stuff."

"I don't have anything to do with the shops."

"Not even as a customer."

"No."

"Weird." He pushed up from the table and looked down at her. "If my family owned those joints, they'd have a hell of a time getting rid of me. I'd be drinking the profits all day."

He walked around her and snagged his heavy sweatshirt out of the hall closet. Yanking it on, he zipped it up and she saw the faded white capital lettering spelling out NAVY. He slapped one hand to his back pocket as if checking for his wallet, then turned and headed for the front door.

Stunned, Kim watched him. He wasn't going to say anything? No caustic jokes about her being rich? No teasing proposal of marriage? No half-joking pleas for an all-expense paid trip to the Bahamas?

''That's it?'' she asked. Now that he hadn't said anything that she'd assumed he would, she was too intrigued to let it go. ''That's all you have to say?''

He stopped with his hand on the doorknob and turned to look at her. ''What were you expecting?''

She pushed her glasses higher up on her nose and stared at him. He'd surprised her. She hadn't seen a glimpse of speculation in his eyes. Not even the slightest sheen of greed. ''I don't know.'' She hedged a bit, not willing to admit that she thought a little better of him for not looking at her and seeing dollar signs. ''Most people want to know how rich I am.''

He shook his head. ''It's none of my business.''

''True,'' she said. ''But that doesn't stop anyone else from asking.''

''Money doesn't mean a hell of a lot to me,'' he said and opened the front door, allowing a wide slash of sunlight to spear into the room. ''If it did, I damn sure wouldn't have joined the navy. Military bank balances are just downright embarrassing.''

She opened her mouth, then closed it again. She

didn't know what to say, so it would be better all the way around if she just kept quiet.

"So," he asked when she simply stared at him, "you want me to bring you some tea?"

After filling up on coffee, Zack kept busy the rest of the day by installing new locks on her doors and windows. Naturally, she'd objected, but he'd reminded her that it was now his job to see to her safety. And damn it, he was good at his job.

He sure as hell hadn't requested this assignment, but now that he had it, he'd do his best.

The window guard locks would never stop a man determined to enter, but it would sure as hell make the task a little more difficult. The dead bolt locks on the front and back doors, however, were strong enough to keep out just about anyone. And as he walked the perimeter of the little house, he told himself it still wasn't enough.

Disgusted, he looked at all the window panes glistening in the afternoon sunlight. Pretty, to be sure. But all it would take was a brick through the glass and whoever was stalking Kim's father would be in her house in an instant. She shouldn't be staying here. She should be in lockdown somewhere if her old man was that worried about her.

But no one had asked his opinion and, he admitted silently, he'd be willing to bet cold, hard cash that Kim would never stand for being pulled out of her house. The woman had a head like a rock.

And a body like a goddess.

"Whoa," he muttered, stepping through the side gate into the tiny backyard. "When you start daydreaming about fish geeks, Zack, old boy," he whispered, "you've been too long at sea."

That was the problem.

He hadn't been with a woman in too damn long. No wonder the doc was looking good. Hell, that one last night on the town with Hula hadn't produced more than drinking and dancing. He should have spent some quality time with a willing female. Then his hormones wouldn't be on overdrive.

It was the only explanation as to why he found himself watching Kim so closely. Or why he'd suddenly decided that glasses slipping to the end of a short, straight nose were so damn sexy.

Still grumbling, he came around the edge of the house and stopped, staring at the garden she'd made for herself. A brick patio with irregular borders drifted in and out of a patch of grass and low-lying shrubs. A few spears of green were beginning to spring from the freshly tilled dirt and he idly wondered what kind of flowers she'd planted. Judging from everything else he'd seen though, he was willing to bet they were tidy blossoms. Probably stood up straight, like little soldiers marching along the edges of the flower beds. They'd have one or two perfectly aligned leaves and would bloom and then die with predictable regularity.

The woman was wound so tight, she practically gave off sparks. Even her refrigerator was ruthlessly organized into food groups. None of which were the least bit appetizing. Plain yogurt for God's sake. Who ate that stuff?

"Who're you?"

He spun around on his heel to face a woman peering over the fence at him. Gray hair stuck out around her head like well-used steel wool and her sharp blue eyes were narrowed suspiciously on him. Her face was wrinkled, lined deeply from too many years in the sun, and her hands, propped on top of the fence, were grubby with dirt.

"Ma'am," Zack said, nodding.

"Your manners are good, boy," she said, "but that doesn't tell me who you are."

"Zack Sheridan, ma'am," he said, stepping closer and holding out his right hand. "I'm a…friend of Kim's. Staying with her awhile."

She grabbed his hand and shook it, transferring a good portion of the dirt clinging to her skin to his. "Friend, is it?"

"Yes, ma'am." He wasn't about to tell someone he'd never met before that he was here as a bodyguard. Probably just a nosy neighbor, but Zack had learned early that it wasn't wise to throw trust around too easily.

"Well, she could use a friend, I'm thinking." The woman nodded. "You just call me Edna, son. It's good to see Kim having a 'friend' over. Alone too much. Not good to be alone. Start talking to yourself and then where'll you be?"

"I—"

"Locked up," she finished it for him. "That's where. Talk to yourself and people start thinking you're peculiar. It's all right when you're old like me. Supposed to be peculiar. People expect it. Colorful. That's what I am."

"Yes, ma'am." Zack grinned. The more she talked, the higher her voice went, as if she was preaching to rows of interested listeners.

"Young people got to get out sometimes. Go to a dance. I'm always telling Kim she should find herself a handsome man. Kick up her heels a little. Looks like she listened, finally." She looked him up and down, then narrowed her steely eyes again. "You see that you take her dancing, you hear?"

"Yes, ma'am." Edna would have made a good admiral. All talk and no listening.

"Good. Now I've got to get my daffodil bed loosened up." She slapped her grubby palms down on the top of the fence. "Nearly spring, you know. Can't wait till the last minute."

"No, ma'am."

When she was gone, Zack chuckled and headed for the back door. But he hadn't gone more than a step or two before he really thought about what Edna had said. So Kim was alone too much, huh? Didn't go out? See people?

Why?

He stopped on the back porch and looked through the window in the door and spotted Kim, still sitting at the tiny table, working on her research. The woman had hardly moved from that spot all day. She flipped through books, rifled through papers and did her best to ignore him— well, except for the glare she'd shot him while he was "making too much noise" installing the locks.

She was pretty much cut off—at least from him. And Zack wondered just why it was a pretty woman like Kim would prefer fish to people.

When the phone rang an hour later, Kim reached for it and, distracted, mumbled, "Uh-huh?"

"Hey, Kim."

"Reid." She dropped her pen and leaned back in her chair. Her older brother's voice was warm and rich and slow, as any good Southerner's would be. Just hearing it made her relax a little. She realized suddenly the day was gone and she'd spent hours hunched over her work. Her back ached and her eyes were throbbing.

Plucking her glasses off, she set them aside and

rubbed her eyes with her fingertips. It wasn't just the day of work that had her tired, though. Having Zack in and out of her house all day had kept her on edge. Even when he was trying to be quiet, she knew he was there. She felt his presence in the room with her and her concentration had been slipping all day. It had taken her twice as long as usual to get half as much work done.

"How are you, Kim?"

She smiled into the phone, despite the unsettling feeling rippling through her. The second oldest of Abraham Danforth's children, Reid was quiet, and just as seriously minded as Kim. Though, she thought, he had lightened up considerably since falling in love with Tina.

"I'm okay. How's my favorite newly engaged person?"

"Fine."

The clipped, one-word answer immediately told Kim something was up. These days, Reid was normally only too willing to be chatty and to let everyone know just how happy he was with Tina. He wasn't an easy man to shake, so when she heard the tightness in his tone, Kim braced herself.

"What's wrong?"

"Thought you should know," her brother said, measuring each word as he spoke it, "Dad got another threatening e-mail."

Kim's stomach twisted, knotted, then coiled into a vicious ache. "Like the last one?"

"Close enough."

Kim's hand fisted on the telephone until her knuckles whitened. Why was this happening? All of a sudden, her family's lives had been thrown into turmoil and nothing was the same anymore.

Zack stepped into the room. She didn't hear him. She *felt* him. Breathing deeply, evenly, she shot him a quick look. Questions filled his eyes, but she couldn't give him any answers yet. She had to hear the rest.

The first threatening e-mail her father received had been short and to the point.

I've been watching you.

Just enough to throw a pall over her father's senatorial campaign—and the family, not to mention her own life into chaos. As far as Kim knew, the police were still investigating. But it wasn't as easy as someone might think to track an anonymous e-mail message. Thanks to technology, stalkers had more freedom than ever to maneuver.

"What did this one say?"

Reid sighed. "Three words. 'You will suffer.'" Signed the same, Lady Savannah."

Fear tickled the back of her neck, then skittered down her spine. One letter might be a crank. This second one was a little more determined. She sighed and looked up as Zack came around to take a seat beside her at the table. Kim didn't even want to think about how much better she felt just having him close by. If she'd been alone in the house, she would have been worried about nightfall and everything that could hide in the dark.

"How's dad taking it?" she asked.

Reid chuckled wryly. "Like you might think. He's all set to tear through the computer himself and track every wire. He's frustrated, angry…"

"And scared?"

"Not so much for himself." Reid blew out a breath that seemed to echo over the phone. "He's really worried about you."

"He doesn't have to be," she said, picking up her pen to doodle mindlessly on the paper in front of her.

Zack plucked the pen from her nervous fingers and closed his hand over hers. She didn't question it. Didn't wonder if it was a good idea or not. She simply folded her hand into his and held on, grateful for the warmth.

Reid sighed and she heard the fatigue in his voice as he said, "Let's not argue that one, all right?"

"You're right. No arguments."

"Dad just wanted me to check and make sure your bodyguard was there. In your house."

"Oh," Kim said, lifting her gaze to Zack's stony features. "He's here."

Holding her hand. Keeping shadows at bay. Making her think things she shouldn't be thinking. Making her feel things that she'd be much better off not feeling.

Yeah, he was there.

He was everywhere.

"Good," Reid said, oblivious to the turmoil churning through his sister. "That'll take one worry off the old man's mind."

Kim nodded and let her own mind wander while her brother continued, telling her about the private protection the Danforths had put in place around Crofthaven, the family home. She imagined the world shrinking. Tightening up into a small, encapsulated ball, with the Danforth family gathered inside and the world locked out.

It wouldn't last.

Couldn't hold.

You couldn't stay apart from the world forever. Sooner or later, that world would find a way through the cracks. And you'd better be able to deal with it.

Zack's fingers tightened on hers as if he'd read her mind and knew that she needed that one extra squeeze of reassurance.

"Let me talk to Zack a minute, will you?" Reid said abruptly.

She stiffened. "There's no reason to—"

"Give me a break, Kim."

Everybody wanted a break. But, it seemed, nobody wanted to give her one. Sighing, she held the phone out to Zack. As he took it, she pulled her hand free of his, instantly missing not only the warmth of his skin, but the sense of connection. "My brother wants to talk to you."

Walking into the kitchen, Kim stared out her window at the street beyond the glass. She'd made her home here. Set up her own life just the way she wanted it. A part of her family, sure, yet separate and distinct. Here she wasn't just one of the Danforths. Here, she was Dr. Kimberly Danforth. She'd worked hard to earn her degree and for the small successes she'd had and the respect she'd acquired from colleagues.

And now it felt as though everything was being threatened. Some anonymous sneak was throwing invisible darts at her father and the ripples of that action were drifting all the way down to her.

And darn it, she wanted it all to stop.

She wanted her life back the way it had been just two days ago.

Kim hardly noticed when Zack came up behind her.

"Your brother's worried."

"They're all worried about me," she said, never taking her eyes off the limbs of the oak tree in the middle of her yard. Sunset streaked the sky with ribbons of gold and crimson, drifting into pink and orange at the edges. Clouds banked in the distance and the twilight breeze ruffled the leaves of the oak, sending its gnarled limbs dancing and swaying.

From two doors down came the regular thump of a basketball bouncing off the Johnson's garage and a snatch of music drifted from a neighbor's open window.

"They don't have to be worried," Zack said softly.

She turned and looked up at him, standing just an inch or two away from her. He was big and solid, and his features were set in lines of stubborn determination. She missed the feel of his hand on hers and that worried her a little. Not enough to wish him gone just now, but enough to make her wonder if things would ever be able to go back to the way they were before he showed up on her doorstep.

Worry and frustration blended together inside her and bubbled to the surface. "I just want this all to go away," she admitted, then lifted one shoulder in a half shrug. "I suppose that makes me a coward."

He leaned one hip on the granite counter and looked down at her. Reaching out, he speared a stray lock of her hair and gently tucked it behind her ear. She shivered lightly as his skin brushed over hers.

"You're no coward," he said, smiling. "You didn't even want a bodyguard, remember?"

One corner of her mouth tilted. "But I've got one, don't I?"

"Damn straight, peaches," he said, his smile carrying the unmistakable sheen of self-confidence. "And as long as I'm here, you don't have to worry, either."

Five

———

The latest threat on her father's life had affected Kim whether she wanted to admit it or not.

Her eyes were haunted, shadows drifting across their grass-green surfaces. She jumped at unexpected noises and darted anxious glances behind her when they were out on her nightly walks.

It bothered the hell out of Zack.

He was forced to stand by and watch, as daily, she became just a little more tightly wound. And for the first time in years, he was unsure about what to do.

Usually, he had no doubts. He had a target and he did what he had to do to accomplish his goals.

But this enemy was nebulous. Hiding in shadows, moving behind the scenes, using fear as a weapon. He felt helpless and he didn't like the feeling.

But he had to admire Kim's handling of the situation. She didn't surrender to the fear. She rose above it, going on with her life as if nothing was wrong. She insisted on keeping up with her routines, refusing to give in to his suggestions to stay close to home—or better yet, get the hell outta Dodge.

He wanted to take her somewhere. Anywhere, really. A safe house. Someplace that no one else knew about. Where whoever was threatening her father would never find her. But she wouldn't go. She'd already made that perfectly clear and he didn't feel like having the same old argument with her again.

"So," he muttered, "how am I supposed to protect her from something I can't see?" He reached for a coffee cup. "Can't hit? Can't stop?"

Damn unsettling for a man used to action to be trapped in a holding pattern that showed no signs of letting up. And the longer they were trapped together in that little house, the crazier she made him. It wasn't only worry that had him walking a razor's edge, delicately balanced between sanity and madness.

It was Kim herself.

Zack groaned and poured himself a cup of coffee from the new coffee maker as he stared out the kitchen window. Gray clouds had scuttled in off the ocean and hung low over Savannah like a cold steel blanket. Wind whipped through the trees and every once in a while, a distant rumble of thunder rolled out like a pack of snarling dogs.

He took a sip of the steaming, rich brew and told himself the weather suited his mood. Grim. Damn it, she was pushing him way beyond the point of no return.

Worse yet, she was doing it without even really trying.

Every night, he stretched out on a narrow day bed she kept in the small second bedroom she used as an office. And every night, he lay awake, listening to the sounds she made during the night. Her damn bed squeaked loud enough to be classified as a scream. When she turned in her sleep, that shriek of sound carried to him and he wondered if she was lying on her back or her stomach? Was she wearing flannel pj's or something silky? Or, God help him, nothing at all?

The wall dividing the two rooms was a flimsy barrier of two sheets of pine paneling nailed to a few two by fours.

Which meant it was no wall at all.

He heard her breathing. He heard her soft sighs and the whisper of bed covers as sheets slid along her body. And he imagined, all too clearly, storming through those flimsy walls and showing her just how loud her bed really could squeak.

He was only averaging a couple hours sleep a night and it didn't do a damn thing for his temperament to know that Kim didn't seem to be bothered by his presence in the slightest.

Just his luck.

The fish geek was getting to him.

And for the first time in memory, the woman he wanted didn't want him.

"Just as well," he muttered and took another sip of the steaming coffee, wincing when he burned his tongue. Kim Danforth wasn't the kind of woman Zack went for. She practically reeked of permanence. He liked his women a little more temporary. He liked going into a relationship knowing that neither he nor the woman in question had any plans for a future.

Three years ago, he'd tried planning a future. An old, tired ache pinged briefly in his heart, then disappeared. He'd thought himself in love, popped the damn question and had his own balloon popped when the lady said no. It seemed a Navy SEAL was good enough to sleep with, but she'd wanted more out of life than a military paycheck and a husband who was gone more than he was home.

The worst of it was, once the hurt had faded, Zack couldn't even blame her for saying no.

Zack had made it a point to keep his distance

from the kind of woman who was currently making him nuts. Revolving-door relationships were a lot easier on the heart. He had no intention of giving up his military career—and really, what kind of life was that to offer a woman? SEAL spouses spent most of their time worrying. Who the hell would readily agree to that?

His gaze focused on his own reflection in the window and he narrowed his eyes at himself. "There's nothing for you here, man. So pull it together already. You've only got three weeks left on this mission. Hell, you can do three weeks."

He'd made it through SEAL training. Finished top in his class. He'd dived in shark-infested waters. He'd had a ship blown up under him. Hell, he'd survived a four-day trek through a desert armed only with a quart of water and a GPS.

Zack straightened up.

"Hoo-yah," he muttered. "You can live through all that, you can live through Kim Danforth."

He turned his back on his own reflection and let his gaze wander the confines of his cozy prison.

His newly purchased coffee maker sat on the gleaming kitchen counter alongside Kim's blender. While she whirled together disgusting concoctions of carrots and peaches and whatever else she found lying around, he enjoyed the rich scent of ground D & D coffee beans being brewed.

She ate plain yogurt and bagels with enough stone-ground wheat in them to be still growing in a field somewhere. He ate frozen waffles dripping with maple syrup.

"Complete opposites," he murmured, underlining their differences as he shook his head. So why, then, did he want her so bad?

"They say talking to yourself is the first sign of dementia."

Her voice, silky, soft, sly, brought him up short.

"There're those big words again," Zack commented and pushed away from the counter. Damn good thing she couldn't read minds.

She gave him a quick smile and he sucked in a gulp of air, hoping to ease the punch of it.

Didn't help.

"So what is it exactly that we're doing today?"

She glanced up at him. "I'm driving to Tybee Island to take some pictures."

"Of?"

"The ocean. Kelp beds. Whatever."

"Is this for your research project?"

"Nope." She straightened, then reached up, gathered her long, black hair into a ponytail at the back of her head and carelessly whipped a rubber band around it. "This is for me."

"Probably not a good idea, Kim," he said.

Her hands dropped to her sides and fisted. "I need to get out of the house, Zack."

"We're still going for those walks at night."
Though he was planning on cutting them down to
a couple of nights a week. Didn't pay to lay down
a routine for a stalker, no matter what she'd like
to think.

"I'm starting to feel like a vampire," she
snapped, then sent him a long look. "I know
you're going stir crazy, too."

"Does feel like the walls are closing in sometimes," he admitted. Although, he'd keep to himself the fact that she was the main reason for his
jumpiness. Hell, he could be on an aircraft carrier
and if she were somewhere aboard, the ship would
feel too small.

"Then let's go." She tilted her head and looked
up at him.

"Gonna storm."

"I won't melt."

Zack stared at her for a long minute. Most
women he'd known wouldn't even think of going
outside without layering on a coat of war paint.
But Kim hadn't even checked a mirror to see if
her ponytail was straight. She didn't have a trace
of makeup on, yet her skin nearly glowed. Her eyes
looked huge with her hair pulled back off her face
and her stubborn chin looked a little more fragile
than usual. Her eyes met his and he saw the skitter
of nerves in their depths and he knew what it was
costing her to hold it together. Maybe she was do-

ing it out of pure stubbornness, but however she was managing it, she was close to the breaking point.

Her gaze drilled into his and he felt that solid punch of awareness hit him low and hard and this time he didn't even flinch. He didn't have a clue as to what to do about his body's response to her...but he sure as hell couldn't seem to stop it.

"What the hell."

She grinned and relief flickered in her eyes just long enough to make him glad he'd relented.

"Thanks."

He grabbed up her black tote bag and his eyebrows lifted. "Weighs a ton."

"Need help?"

"Not likely," he quipped, swinging the straps of the bag up and over his shoulder. Heading to the front porch, he said, "I've carried fully loaded packs through jungles so thick you can't see and so dense you can't take a step without catching your foot on roots bigger than your arm...this little pack is no problem."

"Jungles, huh?" Kim followed him out and stopped to lock the door behind them. "Is that where you were last? I mean before coming here?"

"No," Zack said, remembering that last mission. No jungles. Just hills and forests and rivers and gunfire.

"No? Just no?" She looked up at him. "You can't tell me where you were?"

"I could," he said amiably, taking her elbow in a firm grip as he led her down the steps. "But then I'd have to shoot you. And you're just too damn pretty to shoot."

She stopped and pulled her arm free.

Frowning, he looked down at her. "What?"

"Don't do that."

"Do what?" He waited, wondering what the hell she was talking about. "Already told you I wouldn't shoot you."

"No." She pulled in a sharp breath and blew it out again in a rush. "Not that. Don't tell me I'm pretty."

A cold wind kicked up out of nowhere and tugged a few long strands of black hair free of her ponytail. They whipped across her eyes and she plucked them free with an impatient hand. Thunder rolled in the distance and echoed ominously around them.

Zack shook his head. "Why not?"

"Because I'm not pretty," Kim told him, lifting her chin and looking him dead in the eye. "And I know it. So I'd rather not hear your standard lines or recycled flattery, okay?"

Well, he thought, so much for friendly banter and a nice release of tension. Looked like they were stacking up for a fight. And hell, a fight was as good a way as any to loosen up.

He swung the bag off his shoulder and let it drop to the grass. The equipment inside the bag rattled in protest at the treatment, but he hardly noticed. "I wasn't giving you a line."

"Right." She planted both fisted hands on her hips, cocked her head and glared up at him. "'You're too pretty to shoot.' Good Lord, Zack. That's right up there with 'what's your sign' and 'my wife doesn't understand me.' But you don't even realize you're doing it, do you? It's practically unconscious."

"Now I'm sleepwalking?"

"That's not what I meant."

He glared at her. "Then say what you mean. You usually do."

"Fine." She nodded sharply. "I have a name, you know. It's *Kim*. K.I.M."

His eyes narrowed on her but he kept his voice low, quiet. "You know, I heard that somewhere."

"Funny." Her eyebrows winged up sharply. "I didn't think you knew it."

"Why's that?" Zack couldn't look away. First, it would have been dangerous to not keep an eye on her at the moment. She looked as though she was suddenly mad enough to chew him up and spit him out. But more importantly, she made a hell of a picture in her fury.

Her eyes were giving off sparks. Fire flashed in those green eyes, until they looked like emeralds under a spotlight. She practically shook with the coiled tension inside her. What had he done to get her so damn mad? One minute, she's all smiles, talking about the ocean, the next she's jumping down his throat, kicking and scratching the whole way down.

And what was wrong with him that he liked seeing her so damn mad?

"Because you rarely use my name." She shifted position slightly, folding her arms beneath her breasts and Zack was just male enough to notice the movement. She noticed him noticing and gave a derisive snort. "Women are just interchangeable to you, aren't we?"

"What the hell—"

"It's like we're an all you-can-eat buffet—"

His eyebrows lifted and Kim practically snarled. She'd stepped right into that double entendre.

"You know what I mean," she snapped, then continued before he could speak again. "Blonde, brunette, redhead. Doesn't really matter as long as we have breasts, right?"

"Hold on a damn minute," he countered, looming over her, trying for steely intimidation. It didn't seem to be working.

"No, you hold on. You think I don't notice you calling me peaches or darlin' or honey or sugar?"

She reached out and poked him in the chest with her index finger. ''You think I don't know that it's your way of talking to a woman without actually having to remember her name?''

He inhaled sharply, deeply, and then closed his mouth tightly.

Irritation swelled inside her and mingled with the tension that had been coiled tight in the pit of her stomach for days. She'd felt like a tightrope walker trying to keep her mind on the research project due in little more than three months, while at the same time trying to keep her mind *off* the fact that someone out there was threatening her family.

Then there was the whole Zack issue.

She kept watching him. Couldn't seem to help herself. He was big and handsome and *there* all the time. She knew darn well that she wasn't the type of woman a man like him usually went for. Hadn't she been generally ignored by the male population for years? But that knowledge hadn't stopped her imagination from kicking into high gear when she least expected it.

She imagined his hands on her. She pictured him, sweeping her up into his arms and carrying her off to her bedroom and making her feel all the things she wanted to feel.

But the last time she'd given in to her fantasies, surrendered to her wants, she'd crashed into a wall of betrayal that still stung if she let herself think about it.

So she wasn't about to stand here and let him say things he didn't mean only to have her heart dredge them up in the middle of the night just to torture her.

"I'm not one of your little shore-leave SEAL groupies," she said quietly. She met his eyes, those greenish blue eyes that she spent way too much time thinking about, and told herself not to look away. "I'm not your latest bed warmer and I'd appreciate it if you'd keep that in mind."

"Number one," he said tightly, "I don't have groupies, darlin'. I have women friends. Occasionally, I have lovers...."

She winced. Oh, she really didn't want to think about him with other women. But men like him had women falling at their feet all the time.

"Unlike you," he added, "I actually prefer people to fish."

Her gaze narrowed. "I never said—"

"You had your say, peaches," he interrupted, keeping his gaze locked with hers. "Now it's my turn. If I say I think you're pretty, then I mean it. I don't have to lie to a woman to get her attention."

"No ego problems here," she whispered.

"None at all," he agreed, giving her a quick,

but lethal grin. "You want to believe I'm lying, there's nothing I can do about it."

"Fine," she snapped. "You're not lying. You just need your eyes checked."

He snorted a laugh. "You're a piece of work, babe."

Kim gritted her teeth and swallowed the twinge of pain. Babe. Darlin'. No one had ever called her by an endearment. Not once. And to hear it now, when she knew it meant nothing, tore at her. Stupid, she thought, to let it hurt. To let it disappoint. To wish, even for a moment, that the words had meaning.

She was a scientist.

She, more than anyone, knew that wishes didn't equal facts.

Zack started talking again and she told herself to listen. "For whatever reason, you decided to take a swing at me. Well, I'm not gonna stand here and get skewered because you're mad at Daddy for siccing a bodyguard on you."

That stung, too. Mostly because it was true. "I'm not mad at—"

"The hell you're not. Now who's lying?" Zack countered, grabbing her upper arms and dragging her close as the first few spattering drops of rain pelted them both. "But you know what the main problem is, darlin'?"

"What?" She squeezed the word through a tight

throat and told herself to ignore the blasts of heat skittering through her.

He gave her a slow smile and let his gaze run over her features. ''You want me bad.''

Damn it, he was right.

Lightning flashed, thunder crashed overhead. Rain erupted and drenched them both. Kim blinked up at his watery image, and thought again that he looked like a pirate. Dangerous.

And way too good.

Her blood was boiling despite the damp chill snaking right down to her bones. His fingers dug into her upper arms and felt like ten separate little match heads. Her insides curled up and whimpered, and a low, throbbing ache pulsed in time with her heartbeat.

Her breath caught in her throat, her lungs straining for air she couldn't seem to deliver. His eyes gleamed and even though her vision was blurred, she read the heat in those blue-green depths and shivered in anticipation.

His breath dusted her face as he leaned closer, and closer and—

He grinned, shook his head and let her go. Surprised, Kim stumbled backward.

''Oh, you want me. And you can have me,'' he said, bending down to pick up her bag before giving her a wink and another smile. ''As soon as you admit it.''

He bent down, picked up her bag of equipment and stared at her while the rain pummelled her. Shaking with want and frustration and trembling with a need so huge she hardly knew what to do with it, she watched him walk away from her.

There would be no walk on the beach during a thunderstorm. Instead, they'd be trapped together in a house that seemed to be shrinking daily. It was going to be a long day.

But she could do it. She could survive the wanting. She could be in that house with Zack and never admit just how much she wanted him. She wouldn't give him the satisfaction. Inwardly, she winced as she admitted that she'd be cheating herself of satisfaction as well.

Soaked to the skin, Kim swallowed that regret, stared up at him and said, "It'll be a cold day in hell before I admit any such thing."

Grinning again, he swiped one hand across his face, wiping the water off his skin. "Darlin', it *is* a cold day in hell."

Six

The storm raged outside, trapping them inside. For two hours, the wind howled and rain pelted the windows like thousands of arrogant fists demanding entry. The assault finally ended as the rain became a cold mist and the wind died into a soft moan that sighed around the edges of the house.

Kim curled into one corner of the sofa and balanced a book she wasn't reading on her lap. Her gaze slid from the pages to Zack, staring at the television with all the concentration of a neurosurgeon tackling a brain tumor.

He wasn't fooling her.

She knew darn well he wasn't paying attention

to the mindless chatter spewing from the TV. His hands, fisted on the arms of the chair were a big clue. And the grim set to his mouth. Her gaze fastened on that mouth and she wondered, as she had for the last few hours, just what it would have tasted like. What his mouth would have felt like, pressed to hers. She had a feeling that being kissed by Zack Sheridan was like nothing she'd ever experienced before.

But she wouldn't be finding out anytime soon, since he'd said she'd have to initiate anything between them. And she'd be blasted before she'd inflate his ego that much more.

Still, she wasn't going to sit in silence for the rest of the night, either. It was bad enough having a constant companion foisted on her. A surly, silent companion was even worse.

"Storm's over," she said.

"Thanks for the update." His gaze never left the TV.

Well, that was nice. Scowling at the inane game show, Kim thought, just for a minute or two, about throwing something through the television screen. She happened to know that she was way better company than the idiot woman cooing over a new refrigerator.

"How can you watch that stuff?" she finally blurted.

He slid a long, lazy look at her, swept her up

and down, then settled on her gaze. One dark brown eyebrow lifted. "There some fish show you'd rather be watching?"

She met his gaze and ignored the little jab. "You know, there's no reason why we have to be enemies."

"Nope. No reason. Some things just *are*."

"And that's how you want to leave it?" Kim challenged, watching him. She was sure she saw a flicker of emotion run through his eyes and then disappear.

One corner of his mouth tipped up and Kim's stomach did a quick flip-flop.

"Doc," he said, his voice caressing each word, "I already told you. You want things to change, all you have to do is say so."

Her body jittered with anticipation, but Kim's brain willed it into submission. "I'm never going to—"

He cut her off. "Never say never, darlin'."

She took a deep breath, hoping to quell the fury that nearly blinded her. "You are the most—"

A knock at the door interrupted her and Kim shot to her feet. Anything was better than trying to talk reasonably with a man who was so clearly unwilling to be reasonable.

Edging around the couch, she headed for the door. But Zack moved even more quickly than she did. He stepped in front of her, holding up a hand to keep her back.

"It's probably a neighbor," she muttered.

"Just in case," he said. "I answer the door, got it?"

"For heaven's sake..."

He ignored her muttered complaints, checked the peephole, then laughed and yanked the door open. Kim looked over his shoulder at the men grouped on her porch.

"Hey, boss."

Three men, wearing worn, faded jeans and T-shirts in a variety of colors, stood on the porch, grinning.

"What the hell are you guys doing here?" Zack asked.

"Figured you must be missing us by now," one of them said.

"Like a rash." Zack snorted a laugh.

Amazing. Kim instantly felt the difference in Zack's mood. Pleasure colored his voice and the tension that had been gnawing at him for the last two hours drained away. In the glow of the porch light, the three men stood on her porch, aligned together in a small wave. And they seemed to snake out invisible arms to draw Zack into their center.

The men were clearly military, despite their casual clothes. They stood as if at attention, broad shoulders squared, hands behind their backs. And if that weren't enough, their military buzz cuts screamed out their identities. Zack and these men were more than friends, she thought. They were... family of a sort. Connected by something she'd probably never fully understand.

Zack suddenly seemed to remember that she was there. When he turned to look at her, his eyes were warm and friendly. Unguarded. Their fight earlier and the squabble just moments ago were clearly forgotten. His wide smile drew her into the circle of men, including her, and Kim was grateful.

"Kim," Zack said, sweeping out an arm to indicate all three men, "this is my team. Hula Akiona—"

A tall, dark man with black hair and dark brown eyes grinned at her and nodded. "Ma'am."

"Mad Dog Connelly."

The next man, just as tall, with pale blond hair and deep blue eyes gave her a smile that was both wicked and deceptively innocent.

"And Three Card Montgomery."

"'Lo," the last man said. He was shorter than the others, but with a quiet intensity streaming from his brown eyes.

Kim stared at them all, then shifted her gaze to Zack before saying, "Why don't you all come in and sit down?"

"Thank you, ma'am." Hula said and started inside, leading the way.

"Call me Kim."

"Nice place," Mad Dog muttered as he punched a quick fist into Zack's middle in greeting.

"Don't mean to impose," Three Card whispered, then stepped inside.

Zack looked at her and gave her a smile that made Kim glad she'd gone with her first instincts and invited his friends in. She would have slipped away to her bedroom, to give him some time with his friends, but Zack grabbed her hand and drew her into the living room with him.

"So what's with the visit?" Zack asked.

The men were sprawled comfortably on her furniture and for the first time, Kim realized just how feminine and dainty her surroundings were. These muscular men looked like tigers crouched in cat carriers. One of them was sprawled on her couch, the other draped bonelessly across one of her chairs and the third had plunked down in front of the hearth, where a fire snapped and hissed.

"Wanted to give you the word on Hunter." Three Card spoke up, leaning his forearms on his knees and flipping idly through a magazine on the table in front of him.

"Who's Hunter?" Kim asked no one in particular.

"Hunter Cabot. The last member of our team," Zack said tightly. "How is he?"

"Sitting up and driving the nurses crazy." Hula chuckled and scooted a little farther back on the stone hearth, edging closer to the screened-in fire. "One of 'em's thinking about a sexual harassment suit. A redhead."

"Always his weakness," Three Card said from the chair.

"Then he's gonna be okay," Zack said, relief coloring his voice.

"Got a weakness of your own now, don't you, man?" Hula said, grinning at Three Card.

"Funny."

Zack glanced at Kim. "Three Card just got married a while back."

"Congratulations," Kim said automatically.

The intense man nodded at her. "'Preciate it." He looked at Zack again. "Hunter keeps askin' for his pants and a beer—not necessarily in that order." Three Card reached out one leg and shoved Hula farther to the side. "Shift, man. You're hoggin' the fire."

Hula swatted the man's big foot out of the way and didn't budge an inch. "The doctors are threatening him with restraints."

"Wouldn't hold him, anyway. He's just as ugly and mean as ever," Mad Dog offered.

"What happened to him?" Kim asked, looking from one man to the next.

"Nothing," Zack said tightly.

"Nothing?" she repeated. "Your friend's in the hospital recovering from a bad attack of nothing?"

"Boss is just being modest, ma'am," Hula said.

Mad Dog snorted and gave Hula another good-natured push.

Zack scowled at all of them.

Kim ignored him. "If he's so modest, why don't you tell me," she said and moved around Zack to take a seat on the couch opposite Hula.

"Be happy to, ma'am," the man said, then slid a look at Three Card. "But why don't you get the supplies out of the car first? I'm feeling a little dry."

"Supplies?"

"Beer," Zack muttered.

Three Card vaulted over the back of the sofa in a quick, fluid move, then slipped through the front door. While she was staring after Three Card, Hula started talking. Zack took a seat behind her, on the arm of the couch. His thigh, hard and warm, pressed into her back and Kim leaned into him. She felt Zack shift uncomfortably as his friend talked, telling her about their last mission.

Hula's words painted a vivid picture. The darkness, the danger. She felt their victory when they rescued the hostage and shared in their fury when they were told to leave one of their own behind.

"That's terrible," she blurted.

"Yes, ma'am," Hula said, mouth grim. "That's what we thought."

"Damn politicians," Three Card murmured, as he walked in and set the twelve pack of cold beer atop a magazine in the center of the table. Pulling a few out, he passed them around, first handing one to Kim.

"She doesn't—" Zack started to say.

"Thank you," Kim said and accepted the beer. Lifting the can to her lips, she took a sip and Zack grinned.

"So, what happened?" she asked.

"Hunter's in the hospital," Zack reminded her, "we got him."

"Thank God."

"No, ma'am," Hula said, staring at Zack. "Thank the boss. Shooter told the big guns to go to hell, then he doubled back, scooped Hunter up and carried him out on his back."

"Shooter?" she asked.

"The boss's code name."

"Shut up, Hula."

"Keep talking, Hula," Kim said.

"Yes, ma'am." He grinned at her and ignored Zack. "Shooter carried Hunter out on his back, under enemy fire and got him back to the Zodiac in time to be evacuated.''

''Alone?'' She stared up at Zack and wasn't surprised to see him shift uncomfortably again. She couldn't imagine going into danger alone. Yet he did it all the time. As routinely as she walked to the beach to take photos of starfish.

Pride filled her as she looked up at him. She'd never known anyone like him. The men she'd grown up around would take credit for the simplest of tasks. Hailing a cab in the rain. Landing a successful account. But Zack faced down guns to help a friend and didn't want to be reminded of it. Apparently, he had no problem doing what needed to be done. He simply didn't want to be praised for it. Even if the praise was well deserved.

Three Card laughed. ''Shooter does best on his own, ma'am. It's how he likes it.''

Zack scowled at him.

Kim was fascinated. She'd known that Zack was a warrior. He carried an innate sense of self-confidence that she envied. She'd never really been sure of herself. Oh, she was confident in her work. She knew oceans and marine life. But put her on dry land and throw her into a situation where she'd be forced to talk to people and she was lost. At parties she could be most often found standing in a corner, talking to a plant. Or better yet, sneaking out early and heading back home. To her nest. Her cave.

Her sanctuary.

At least, that's what it had been until Zack had invaded it. And now, she doubted that it would ever feel the same to her again. He'd imprinted himself on the walls. He'd made himself a part of her daily life and she wasn't sure how to get him back out again.

Or even if she wanted to.

"You saved him." She looked up at Zack until he met her gaze and when he did, she saw embarrassment color his eyes. Something she hadn't expected. And for some reason, she liked him even more for it.

"The team goes in," he said simply, "the team comes out."

"Hoo-yah," the three other men muttered all at once, lifting their bottles of beer in salute.

The evening slid past in a rush of conversation and laughter. Forgotten, the TV provided a background current against the ebb and flow of stories being told. Kim laughed and talked more than she had in years. The men, closer than brothers, teased and joked and drew her into their camaraderie, made her one of them, and she loved it. She felt a sense of belonging that she'd never really felt before. She drank beer until her head swam, and then she ate pizza. She hadn't had pizza in years, but when Hula had two huge pies delivered, she'd dug right in with the rest of them, fighting and grumbling over every slice of pepperoni.

It felt...good. It felt comfortable. She felt Zack's approval as he watched her fit in with his friends.

By the time she was on her fourth beer, the stories had turned to scuba diving and they were all recounting their favorite spots. Here, Kim joined right in, telling her own version of war stories.

These men understood her love of the sea. The dangers and the attractions of visiting a world far below the surface of the everyday. They'd seen the beauty and experienced the unbelievable silences of deep-water diving. They knew what she knew. They'd each known the magic of descending into darkness and finding life teeming around them in the frigid waters.

"Oh, man, here's the best part," Hula shouted, splintering conversations and grabbing everyone's attention at once.

"What?" Kim turned her head too quickly and saw the room spin. Probably not a good thing.

"The movie—" Hula pointed to the TV and Three Card groaned.

"The man never gets tired of this."

"Tired of what?" Confused, Kim blinked to bring the men into focus, then turned her gaze on the television set where an old movie was playing.

The characters were sitting around a scarred table aboard a disreputable boat in the middle of the ocean. Drinking themselves silly, they were comparing scars as a giant shark circled their small ship, looking for revenge.

"I can beat them," Hula said and lifted his left leg, propping one foot on the edge of the table. Pulling his jeans up, he displayed a vicious scar. "Barracuda, Florida Keys."

"Hell," Three Card said, then winced. "'Scuse me, ma'am. That's nothin'." He stood up, lifted the tail of his shirt and displayed a flat, tanned abdomen with a circular scar over his ribcage. "Tiger Shark, Gulf of Mexico."

Kim grinned as Mad Dog rolled the right sleeve of his shirt up. Slapping one hand to the long, thin scar wrapping around his bicep, he proclaimed, "Stingray, Malibu."

Zack, not to be outdone, pulled his shirt up and turned around, exposing the long scar waving across the small of his back. "Moray eel, Thailand."

Four pairs of eyes shifted to Kim in silent challenge. She thought about it for a long minute, then decided, she was a part of this group, now. They'd welcomed her in, and now she could pay her dues. Propping her left leg up on the coffee table in front of her, she pulled up the hem of her jeans and displayed a set of small, circular scars running up the inside of her calf. "Octopus, Sea of Japan."

"Hoo-yah!" all four men cried, lifting their beers in a salute to her.

Kim grinned and for the first time in her life, felt as though she really belonged.

Hours later, Zack was stretched out on his narrow bed, staring at the ceiling. The guys were long gone in the cab Zack had called for them. Kim was tucked up in her soft bed and every time she shifted, he winced at the creak of her bedsprings.

Watching her all night, it had taken everything in him not to grab her and kiss her senseless. He never would have believed that the fish geek would pull up the leg of her jeans and match scars with a bunch of SEALs. Miss Whole-Wheat-Bagels-and-Blended-Carrot-Juice had sucked down beer and fought him for the last slice of pizza. She'd laughed and told stories and that grin of hers had hit him hard enough that his heart was still a little rocky.

She'd made him want her more than ever.

Damn it.

From the room next door, the bed creaked again and Zack told himself not to think about it. He closed his eyes, but that didn't help, since he kept seeing her in his mind, smiling up at him.

"Zack?"

His eyes flew open. Turning his head to the wall, he stared at the paneling as if he had X-ray vision. "Yeah?"

"I like your friends," she said, her voice clear and soft through the wall that wasn't a wall at all.

He scrubbed one hand hard across his face. "They liked you, too."

"They did, didn't they?"

Frowning now, he said, "That surprises you?"

A long pause before, "Well, yeah."

"Why?"

"You don't like me. I figured they wouldn't, either."

"I never said I didn't like you."

"Do you?"

He pushed himself up onto one elbow and stared at the damn wall. "Why am I talking to a wall if I don't?"

"I like you, too," she said after another long moment. "I didn't think I would, but I do."

"Thanks." He's dying of want and she "liked" him. That was just great.

"If I tell you something, will you promise to stay where you are?"

"I never make promises without all the facts," he said, dropping his head back onto the pillow. The ceiling tiles were dotted with thirty-four speckles of green paint and seventy-five speckles of gray paint and one hundred and twenty-seven dots of blue paint. He knew. He'd counted them all in the last two hours. Desperate to get his mind off Kim, he'd resorted to math, for God's sake.

And now she wanted to have a heart-to-heart chat from behind the safety of a sheet of paneling?

"Just promise," she said and he heard her teeth grinding.

"If it'll get you to shut up and go to sleep, I promise."

Seconds ticked past. Wind kicked up outside and rattled under the eaves of the old house.

"You were right before," she said finally, her voice softer now, a little more hesitant.

"I never get tired of hearing a woman say that to me, Doc," he said, smiling a little. "But right about what, exactly?"

"Earlier today," she said. "When we were outside?"

His insides coiled, tightened. "Yeah?"

"You said I wanted you."

"And…"

"You were right."

Kim's bedroom door flew open and Zack was silhouetted in the open doorway. She shot straight up in bed, clutching the rose-patterned quilt to her chest. Glaring at him, she shouted, "You promised to stay in your own room!"

"I lied."

Seven

Kim leaped off the bed, dragging the sheet and quilt with her. Clutching both to her chest, she stared at him in dumbfounded shock and... appreciation.

He was really built. His muscled, well-defined chest gleamed like warm, golden honey in the slash of moonlight spearing through her room. The waistband of his jeans hung open, giving her a tantalizing glimpse of slightly paler flesh. Deliberately, she looked away and lifted her gaze to his.

"You said you never lied."

"Not about the big things."

She nodded her head sharply. "This is pretty big."

He grinned quickly, devastatingly. "Thanks."

Kim's stomach quivered even while her sense of humor tickled. "I didn't mean that."

One dark eyebrow lifted.

She scooped her hair back with an impatient hand. "You're impossible."

"It's been said before."

"Oh, I'm sure of that." She inhaled deeply and blew out a surprisingly shaky breath. He was so much more than she'd expected. So much more dangerous a man than she'd ever known before.

Not dangerous physically, of course. But the threat to her heart kept growing. She didn't want to care about him. Didn't want to feel anything for a man she knew was only there because he'd been ordered to protect her. And she knew that the moment his "sentence" was lifted, he'd be gone. She'd be a memory and he'd be on to the next woman.

And despite that, a part of her wanted to cross the room, step into his arms and enjoy what he was offering, anyway. But a larger and, she hoped, smarter part of her knew better. The line between brains and desire was blending, though, and if she didn't act quickly, it'd be too late to stop the inevitable. Lifting one arm, she pointed at the doorway and said simply, "Out."

He didn't budge. "I'm not in yet."

God, he could affect her this much and he

wasn't even within reach. What would he be able to do if he actually got his hands on her? *Oh, boy.* Her blood did a quick boil and her breath staggered from her lungs. "You're not going to be in, either."

He gave her a slow, lazy smile. "You said you wanted me."

Oh, yeah, she thought. Big-time. "I want lots of things."

He grinned. "I'll see what I can do."

"Cut it out, Zack."

He put one hand against the doorjamb and leaned his weight into it. His chest rippled and Kim sucked in a breath. But the air in the room felt thick and hot and she couldn't seem to make her lungs work.

He took a step into the room and Kim's heart skittered in her chest.

His gaze drilled into hers and even in the darkness, she saw the heat, the desire, the glint of pure need shining in their depths. "All teasing aside," he said, his voice soft and warm, "I want you to know, I didn't technically lie."

She opened her mouth to argue, but he kept talking.

"It's important to me that you know I won't lie to you."

"You're here. You promised to stay in your own room."

He smiled and shrugged slightly. "A promise made under duress."

"Duress?"

"And I had my fingers crossed."

She laughed shortly. "What are you, twelve?"

"Only in my heart," he said, smiling.

"Right."

"So, we're clear on the not-lying thing?"

Kim looked at him closely and saw that despite the teasing note in his voice, his eyes were dead serious. This was clearly important to him and the fact that it was meant a lot to Kim. "We're clear."

"Good." He took another step closer to her and stopped. "Now. About the other thing."

"Yes?"

"I told you before that you'd have to ask."

"I know." Her voice sounded creaky, unused, as if she'd been mute for years and was only now attempting speech. She swallowed past the knot in her throat and told herself to get a grip. But it wasn't easy when everything in her ached. Need pumped through her body, leaving flash fires in its wake. Her knees went weak and her blood pumped in a furious rush, making her head spin.

If she had any sense at all, Kim thought, she'd tell him to leave again, and this time, she'd mean it. But while her brain argued with her hormones, Kim couldn't help thinking, *why not?*

They were adults. There was an obvious attraction. Neither one of them was looking for anything more than an end to the need rocketing around the room like a Ping-Pong ball. There was an easy answer to all this. All she had to do was make a move and she could feed the fires within. She could enjoy Zack and then have her life back when he was gone.

All she had to do was speak up.

So what was stopping her?

Reality, that's what. She took a deep breath in a desperate attempt to steady herself, but since that was useless at this point, she simply started talking.

"Okay, I can admit this much."

His eyes darkened, his mouth tightened, but he didn't speak. He waited.

"I do want you."

"Atta girl," he muttered and started around the edge of the bed.

"But..." That one single word had the desired effect. It stopped him cold.

"How did I know that was coming?" he asked, shaking his head.

"Maybe you're the psychic."

"Yeah, that's it."

"There has to be a 'but,' Zack," she said, clutching the quilt and sheet just a little closer to her chest.

"With you?" he murmured. "Naturally."

"What's that supposed to mean?" she demanded.

He held both hands up, palms out. "Cool down, Doc. All I meant was, there's nothing about you that's easy."

Kim smiled as her temper eased and the feelings she'd expected would be stomped on were instead soothed. "I think that was a compliment, Zack."

A long moment passed before he nodded. "Yeah, I guess it was."

"Thanks." Warmth stole through her, softer, gentler than the heat that had burst through her body only moments before. That flash fire of need and hunger was exciting, but this slow slide of warmth was more…tempting somehow. More… intoxicating.

Which meant she was in serious trouble. "I'm really tempted to just have an affair with you," she blurted.

"Go with your urges, babe."

"That's what you do, isn't it?" she asked, tipping her head to one side as she watched him.

"Mostly, yeah." He grabbed hold of the spindle post at the end of her bed. Even in the moonlight, she could see his fingers tighten around the carved wood until his knuckles whitened.

"I don't," she said softly. "Not any more. I did once," she offered, knowing that it wasn't what he wanted to hear. "I followed my impulses and they led me right over a cliff."

"Doesn't have to be that way again."

"Maybe not." The more she talked, the stronger she felt. She continued, not knowing if she was trying to explain her decision to him—or to herself. "But that's not how I live. I like things… organized. Tidy."

"And I like 'em loose."

"I know. And God help me," she admitted, shaking her head, "that's part of your appeal."

One eyebrow lifted again.

"How do you do that?"

"Huh?"

"The one-eyebrow lift. How do you—" she broke off, laughing and hoped it didn't sound nearly as hysterical as it felt. "Never mind. Zack, a part of me wants to tell you yes."

"And the other part?"

Kim blew out another breath and lifted her chin. "That part's hoping you'll leave fast before the less-disciplined part takes over."

"Uh-huh." He let go of the bedpost and walked toward her, one slow step after another.

God, just watching him move made her mouth go dry. He was all lean muscle and sharp angles. He moved quietly, as if stepping through a mine-field and maybe, she told herself, he was.

There was nowhere to back up to. Nowhere to

hide. Kim knew if he touched her, all of her fine resolutions and discipline were going to jump out the window, shouting, "Hallelujah," as they went.

"I meant what I said." Zack was close enough now that she could feel the heat pulsing off his body. Waves of hunger and need reached out from him to find her own hunger and need, to stoke them, and they really didn't need any assistance in reaching bonfire proportions.

"Meant what?"

"You'll have to ask." He reached up, stroked her cheek with the backs of his fingers. His touch sent jagged bolts of something deliciously wicked to the center of her belly.

Oh, boy.

"I can't."

"Not now, I see that," he whispered, and he was so close, his breath dusted her cheek as gently as his fingertips had. "But you will."

She stiffened at his cool confidence, but if she were going to be honest, then she had to admit that he was right. Sooner or later, she was bound to cave in. Zack Sheridan at his most lethal was something no woman could resist for long.

Steeling herself against the dazzling light in his eyes, she met his gaze and tightened her grip on the quilt clutched to her and ignored the cool breeze slipping through the partially opened window. Wind chimes danced musically and, from somewhere down the street, a dog barked as though chasing away a horde of invaders.

"It would be easy to give in to what I'm feeling for you."

One corner of his mouth tipped up. "There's another 'but' coming, I can almost hear it."

She obliged him. "But I went with easy once and in the end, it was more difficult than anything I'd ever experienced, before or since."

"What happened?"

His voice was a hush. Like a whisper in a confessional and maybe it was that tone—maybe it was the quiet of the moonlight—that had her telling him what he wanted to hear.

"Charles Barrington the third," she said.

He snorted.

Kim appreciated the sentiment. "He gave me a big rush. Came to the house all the time to see me. Made nice with my brothers, my parents. He brought me flowers, took me to plays and," she said with a sigh, "in general, played the part of the perfect boyfriend."

"When?"

"Hmm?" She was staring at the past and hardly heard her present.

"When was Chuck your man of the moment?"

"Chuck?" Kim slapped one hand across her mouth to muffle the hoot of laughter. "Oh, my

God, Chuck. I never thought, but that's the official nickname for a Charles, isn't it?''

Zack folded his arms over his chest and nodded. His mouth tight, eyes narrowed, he said, ''Now imagine what nasty little four-letter word it rhymes with.''

A moment. Then Kim laughed again. ''Appropriate. Funny how I never thought of that before.''

''Doesn't matter. Tell me about Chuck. Since he's the guy standing between us at the moment, I figure I rate an introduction.''

Her smile slipped away. She felt it and didn't even try to retrieve it. Kim was long over the pain, but she had a feeling that the sting of humiliation, of betrayal, would stay with her to her dying day.

''He asked me to marry him.''

''You said yes?''

''Of course.''

He snorted again.

''What?''

''Nothing,'' he said. ''Just go on.''

''Not much more to tell.'' She shrugged and the quilt dipped near her shoulder. She tugged it back into place. ''We were engaged. Everyone was pleased. Such a good match. Old Savannah families. His father was a congressman, mine was thinking even then about a run for the Senate.''

''And?''

''And,'' she let her gaze drift from his. She

stared out the window into the moonlit backyard and looked instead at the moment that was still carved into her memory. "We were at a party, but I had a headache. Wanted Charles to take me home. But I couldn't find him. No one had seen him for a while."

She closed her eyes now and saw again the brilliantly lit dance floor, the acres of crystal glinting in the overhead lights. Saw the flash of diamonds around the necks of society matrons, heard the whisper of conversations drifting just beneath the dance music provided by a small orchestra at the end of the room.

Kim remembered making her way outside. She could almost smell the jasmine, feel the wet heat of the summer air.

"What happened when you found him?" Zack prompted.

Kim opened her eyes and strangely, she was comforted by Zack's presence, even though she was standing there in little more than her bed clothes.

"I heard voices coming from the gazebo. I walked across the grass, and heard Charles speaking, but I couldn't make out who was with him." She stiffened then, as the memory sharpened, like a cleaver, slicing through her heart again. Thank heaven, the slice it took this time was a lot smaller than it had been once. "When I was close enough,

I heard Charles, carefully explaining to Elizabeth Coopersmith—''

''Where do they get these names?'' Zack reached out and took her hand.

She chuckled at his exasperation and had to admit she felt better for telling him this story. His grip was warm and strong and steady and she was grateful for it. Stupid really, to still feel the sharp slap of humiliation, but there it was.

She swallowed hard and pushed the rest of the words out, wanting it said. ''Charles was telling Elizabeth that once he and I were married, he and Elizabeth could meet again. Seems he'd purchased her a condo outside Hilton Head and she was pouting because he hadn't been by to see what the decorator had accomplished.''

''Bastard.''

She smiled. ''Oh, yes.''

''Did you hit him?''

Kim sighed. ''Why didn't I think of that?''

''I don't know,'' he teased and she turned to look up at him. ''You didn't have any trouble dusting me that night you tried to sneak past me.''

Her lips quirked and the tiny stab of pain eased back into the shadows where it usually stayed. ''Yes, but I was too much the lady that night for anything so unseemly.''

''Too bad.''

''Yes, it is a shame.''

"So what did you do?"

"Oh, I walked into the gazebo, handed Charles his ring back—it was a gaudy thing—and wished him and Elizabeth well."

"Darlin', you let him off easy."

"Not so easy," she said with a shrug of nonchalance she didn't quite feel. "He married her. Believe me, he's paying."

"So you just walked away?"

"It wasn't that civilized," she said. "After all, Charles made a point of telling me he'd been counting on the Danforth money. And that was why he'd put up with the cold fish that I was." She lifted her chin in defiance to an old memory. "Elizabeth had a few things to say as well, since she too had plans for my money—not that her family was poor, you understand. Just—"

"Not as rich as yours."

"Exactly."

"Hmph. Who knew that rich people can come from the wrong side of the tracks, too?"

Kim gave him a small, tired smile. "Not wrong exactly," she corrected, "just less right."

"Oh, yeah, that makes sense."

"Oh, I never said it made sense." She folded her arms across her chest and gave herself a hug.

Zack's insides fisted even tighter than his hands. He wanted to hunt down the miserable bastard who'd broken something fragile inside Kim. He wanted to beat the son of a bitch within an inch of his life, then heal him and start all over again.

But he couldn't do any of that. Charles the third was out of Zack's reach. But Kim wasn't. Her expression and the old sorrow in her eyes pulled at him until it yanked something from him he hadn't really been sure existed.

Tenderness.

"Chuck was a moron."

She laughed sharply. "True."

"So consider the source when you think about anything the idiot had to say."

"Oh, I do. Usually."

"Good. Cold fish?" He shook his head. "You're no fish, peaches," he said and grinned when her mouth flattened into a firm line. She really hated it when he called her anything but Kim. So he'd tease her by giving her something to be mad at. Something to replace the misery of the memory she'd just lived through again.

Reaching over, he cupped her face in his hands and stroked her high cheekbones with the pads of his thumbs. The feel of her skin against his was a jolt of liquid heat that rolled through him like a summer storm sweeping across the ocean.

"Not a damn thing cold about you, darlin'," he said, swallowing hard to choke his own need back.

"If ol' Chuck couldn't find the fire, maybe it was because he didn't have good enough kindling."

She trembled under his touch, his words, and Zack felt that slight reaction shudder through him. This woman had some strong weapons. Weapons she was using effectively whether she was aware of it or not.

"Zack…"

"Me," he said, interrupting her quickly, "I'm a great little fire-starter. But I think your fires burn plenty hot enough without help."

She shook her head, confused now as his words swirled around her and his hands continued to stroke her face. Regret shadowed the want in her cool green eyes and he knew they wouldn't be doing what he'd like to be doing. At least not tonight.

"I can't do this," she said softly.

"I know that," he said, feeling his own aching regret reach up to grab hold of his throat. "I'm just saying, don't let that bastard be the ruler you measure yourself by."

"I don't. I haven't. Not for a long time."

"Good."

"You're not what I expected," she said, her voice as quiet and steady as the beat of her heart, pulsing at the base of her throat.

"Yeah?" he asked, smoothing his hands into her hair, pushing it back from her face. It felt cool and soft as his fingers threaded through the long strands. He wanted to wrap them around his hands, pull her tightly to him and kiss her until neither one of them could think. ''Is that a good thing or a bad thing?''

She sighed heavily then chewed on her bottom lip. ''I think…it's a dangerous thing.'

He chuckled, though it was strained. ''Lucky for you, there's a SEAL in the house. Nothing we like better than danger.''

''Lucky me.'' She gave him a wry smile, then turned her green eyes to him. Her eyes were remarkable. Within their depths he could see her emotions and deep dreams. And he could see himself reflected there, too.

A part of Zack wanted to turn and bolt for cover. He'd never planned on being a part of someone's dream. Didn't know if he could. But damn, if she wasn't the one woman who could make him think about trying.

''I'm uh…gonna go back to my room,'' he said, congratulating himself on being able to speak at all.

She nodded as he stood back, letting his hands fall to his sides. ''Probably safest that way.''

''Not the most fun, though,'' he quipped and gave her another smile, hoping she couldn't see what it cost him to turn and walk away from her.

''Probably not.''

''I'm not him, you know,'' Zack said, his voice

a low scrape of sound. "I don't give a good damn about your money or your family or, God help us, *society.*"

She laughed lightly and it sounded like the crystal ring of the wind chimes hanging outside her window. "I know."

"Okay then," he said, backing up another step and then another until he'd rounded her bed and was safely at her door. "There is one thing you could do for me," he said, one hand on the doorknob, ready to shut himself out and away from her.

"What's that?"

His gaze dropped to the quilt she still held like an ancient shield in front of her. "It's been killing me for a week now, wondering just what you sleep in."

Surprise lit her eyes and, just for a moment, he saw a flash of excitement. "That's probably not a good idea."

"Probably not."

She thought about it for a long moment, long enough to have Zack imagining all kinds of wonderful things. Then she shook her head and that long, black hair flew back from her face. "Why don't we just leave it to your imagination, okay?"

He didn't know if he was disappointed or relieved. Though he'd love to get a look at the woman behind that quilt, he was willing to admit that if he did, it would make sleeping even harder than it was already.

"Doc," he assured her, "my imagination's what's killing me."

"Good night, Zack."

"For some of us," he said, shaking his head. Then, groaning, as the imagination she'd sentenced him to took over, he closed the door with the last of his strength.

Eight

To say things were a little tense around Kim's house would be like describing Mount Everest as a nice little hill.

It had been three long days since Kim and Zack had stood opposite each other in the moonlight, separated only by an antique quilt. And every minute of every one of those days, Kim's mind had reminded her of what she'd turned down.

And Zack wasn't helping any.

She felt him watching her. Felt his gaze on her as surely as she would his touch. He hadn't made a move on her since that night, and she wasn't sure if she was grateful or not. Which was so absolutely contrary, it infuriated her.

But she was walking a fine line between desire and logic. She felt on edge, as if every cell in her body was humming with an electrical charge. Her brain kept telling her that this would pass, and her body wanted her brain to shut up so it could get busy.

Bottom line though, neither of them was happy.

"Nice to find out at the ripe old age of twenty-eight that you're schizophrenic," she muttered to herself, staring unseeing at the landscape whizzing past the window of Zack's shiny black SUV.

"You say something?"

"No." Nothing she wanted to repeat.

"So why are we doing this again?"

She glanced at Zack and really tried not to sigh. But even her stoic mind had to allow her body to respond to Zack Sheridan in dress whites. In the dim light of the dashboard, he looked…way too good. She'd been attracted to the man in jeans and T-shirts. That same man in a dress white uniform was enough to make her want to stretch herself across the hood of the car and shout, "Take me now!"

"It's an engagement party for my brother Reid and his fiancée, Tina." And she'd almost forgotten all about it in the rush of hormones these past few days. What kind of sister did that make her?

"So it's a family thing, then?"

She looked at Zack and chuckled. "Oh, no. That's not the Danforth way, silly man."

"Yeah? What is the Danforth way?"

"Have a party, invite the world." Kim remembered too many of the stiff, formal affairs. Even as kids, she and her brothers had been expected to make an appearance at their parents' parties. They'd troop into the ballroom dressed to the teeth, smile, look like happy, all-American children, pause to be admired briefly, then be trotted off by the nanny, sent back to their rooms to have dinner on a tray.

Even birthday parties had become business deals. Mergers were made while professional clowns entertained society's children. Tonight, Kim knew, would be a different kind of circus— but just as crazy.

"It's a family celebration," she said, "but with dad running for the Senate, he's not about to miss the chance to do a little fund-raising. Reporters will be there and probably a couple of TV cameras." She looked at Zack. "The movers and shakers of Georgia will be filling Crofthaven tonight."

"So," he said, shooting her a quick grin, "I shouldn't be expecting a keg out on the patio?"

She laughed and some of the dread for the coming ordeal fell away. Kim loved her family, but she loathed these performances. She'd always hated the formal gatherings at the Danforth mansion.

Small talk with people you didn't like and wouldn't see again until the next "must" appearance...smiling when your feet hurt, holding a single glass of champagne but not drinking it because it wouldn't do for a Danforth to drink too much. Strained dinner conversations with strangers. No matter how many times she'd done it, she'd never felt comfortable.

"No kegs, but we'll raid the kitchen." She reached out and laid one hand on his forearm. "Joyce, the housekeeper, is a magician. She'll find us a couple of beers."

"Us?" he asked, smiling, moving one hand off the wheel to give her smaller hand a squeeze. "One night of beer and pizza with a bunch of SEALs has turned you off fine wine?"

The heat of his touch slipped right through her flesh and into her bones. It skimmed up the length of her arm and burned warmly in her chest. Reluctantly, she pulled her hand free of his and told herself to pay no attention to the sudden chill she felt.

"Not completely, but I will admit, there's a lot to be said for beer and pizza."

"There's still time to head to Pino's instead."

"Tempting," she said, thinking of the small pizza parlor not far from her house. She sighed inwardly. Oh, yes, Pino's sounded wonderful. "Unfortunately, I'd never hear the end of it."

"Okay," Zack said, shooting her a glance. In the pale light of the dashboard and the occasional flash of oncoming headlights, she looked tense— as though her innerspring had been wound way too tight.

He felt anxiety rippling off her in cool waves. Whether she knew it or not, she was building fences between them. Correction, he thought. She was adding height to the fences already there. The closer they got to the Danforth family mansion, the more reserved she became. It was as if she were slowly turning into a different person. Retreating from the Kim he knew to become the Kimberly who would probably never think of entering a run-down pizza joint.

"Turn right here," she said, and he noticed her voice had dropped another notch.

He steered the car right and passed through an open set of scrolled iron gates with a twin *D* in the center of each. Zack shook his head and guided the car through a long, tree-shaded drive. Moonlight speared down through the trees like an overhead spotlight focusing on a stage. Long, naked fingers of the trees seemed to reach out for the car, and the sheets of moss hanging from the gnarled limbs looked like ghosts, fluttering in the cold ocean wind.

"Impressive," he muttered, keeping his gaze locked on the illuminated path created by his headlights, slicing through the darkness. Far in the distance, he made out the golden sheen of lamplight winking from windows.

She sighed. "You ain't seen nothin' yet."

"Bet this used to intimidate the hell out of your dates back in high school."

"It would have, I suppose, if I'd had any. I went to an all-girls' school. In Switzerland." Her hands clenched more tightly, her fingers pressing against each other until her knuckles whitened. "Not a lot of dating there."

"Pillow fights, though, right?" he asked, grinning, trying to make her smile.

Her mouth lifted briefly and he felt like a hero. "Do all guys think like you?"

"The lucky ones," he said, then shifted his gaze back to the road.

And slammed on the brakes.

"What?" Kim flew forward, was stopped by the shoulder harness, then flopped back against her seat.

"You okay?" Zack asked, even as he unhooked his belt and opened his car door.

"I'm fine. What're you—"

"Don't you see her?" He lifted one hand and pointed to the woman standing at the side of the road. She'd moved out of the center of the drive, where she'd been only moments before. She'd scared hell out of him. Now she was just standing there, her long, black dress sweeping the ground, her pale face turned to them, her dark eyes watching.

"Zack…" Kim glanced at the woman, then back at him. "Let's just go on, okay?"

"Can't just leave her here," he said sharply and climbed out of the car. "Ma'am," he called as he stepped a little closer to the woman. "We'd be happy to give you a ride up to the house."

She gave him a small, brief smile and swayed slightly, as though buffeted by the breeze shooting down the long, tree-lined drive. She was illuminated by the moonlight, but his car's headlights seemed to shine right through her. The woman's long, dark hair lifted in the cold wind and swirled around her face. She lifted one hand to smooth it down, then stared at Zack through eyes dark and shadowed with pain so staggering, he felt the weight of her agony.

Zack's heart jumped to his throat and he wasn't sure why. Something was wrong. The hairs at the back of his neck lifted and sent an icy roll of dread trickling down his spine.

She opened her mouth and spoke. But she made no sound. Zack saw her mouth moving as she tried repeatedly to tell him something she obviously felt was important. She wrung her hands and a solitary tear snaked its way down her cheek as she realized he couldn't hear her.

And the more she tried to make Zack understand, the more her dark eyes filled with frustration. A sense of sorrow so strong reached across the distance to Zack and shook him right down to his bones.

"Zack," Kim said quietly, from behind him.

He couldn't tear his gaze from the woman in front of him, but a part of him clung to the sound of Kim's voice. "You see her, right?"

"Yes."

That was something, then, he told himself. He'd faced guns, mines, storms at sea and more life-threatening situations than most people ever encountered. But standing here in the cold night air watching a ghost made him grateful to have company.

As he watched, the image of the woman wavered, her eyes wept. She shimmered in the dappled moonlight, then slowly disappeared.

Kim would have seen that, too, he told himself. So at least he wasn't headed to the loony bin alone. If they locked him up, maybe Kim would get the cell next door.

He lifted both hands and rubbed them briskly over his face. Then he turned and looked at Kim as she climbed back into the car. She didn't look the least bit surprised by all this. In fact, he remembered, when they'd first seen the woman, she'd told him just to drive on. She'd known that woman was—what...*dead?*

Zack cut that thought off, moved quickly to the car, jumped in and latched his seatbelt. Then, gripping the steering wheel in both fists, he shot her a level look. "What the hell was that?"

"That," Kim said, "was Miss Carlisle."

He thumped the heel of his hand against his ear as if he couldn't quite believe what she was saying. "You know her name?"

"That's all we know about her," Kim told him as he fired up the engine and put the car back into Drive. "Well, that and the fact that she's been dead about a hundred years."

Zack snorted. This was turning out to be one interesting assignment. A gorgeous fish geek, mansions, stalkers and ghosts. And the month wasn't even half over.

Gritting his teeth, Zack blew out a breath and tossed one last look at the drive behind him—at the spot where the woman had disappeared. Nothing. He sent Kim another quick look before starting down the long road again. "So far, it's a hell of a party."

The gathering was everything Kim had expected it to be. Music drifted through the house, a lovely, soft layer just beneath the murmur of well-bred conversations. People wandered across the marble

foyer and gathered at the foot of the circular stair-
case that led to the upper floors. Crowds loitered
in the sitting room where a fire danced and leaped
in the stone hearth. A few people were clustered
in the music room, sitting at the Steinway, while a
very untalented man sat plinking out a melody that
was jarring in contrast to the orchestral melodies
floating on the air. Dozens of silent servers
threaded their way through the crush of people,
carrying silver trays filled with champagne flutes
and elaborate finger foods.

Kim headed for the ballroom, smiling at people
as she passed, but always conscious of Zack's hand
at the small of her back. She concentrated on the
warmth of his fingers, burning through the black
silk of her dress to imprint themselves on her skin.
The feel of him, so close, reminded her that she
wasn't here alone. That she needn't be resigned to
a corner tonight. That the plants surrounding the
polished teak dance floor would have to find someone else to talk to them.

"Lot of people for a family party," Zack muttered, leaning forward until his breath brushed the
back of her neck.

She shivered at the sensation and glanced back
at him. He was close enough for her to feel as
though she were falling into his eyes. Close enough
that a kiss was only a heartbeat away. Kim swal-

lowed hard and did a quick mental retreat. "No Danforth party is ever just family."

He slid his hand around her body to rest on the curve of her hip. Kim sucked in a breath and held it before letting it slide slowly from her lungs. She savored the sensation of his hand on her body even as she spotted envious stares from the women they passed.

Tall and lean and gorgeous, Zack Sheridan was every woman's fantasy in that naval uniform. And for tonight, at least, he was hers.

They paused at the threshold of the ballroom. Zack tensed behind her. She couldn't blame him. She'd grown up in this place and the ballroom could still take her breath away.

A cavernous room, the pale blue walls were decorated with paintings her family had been collecting for generations. In the spring and summer, the French doors on the far side of the room would be thrown open, allowing the scents of roses and jasmine to flavor the air.

But February was chilly even in Savannah. Light from the crystal chandeliers dazzled the crowd and seemed to sparkle through the room as brightly as the diamonds glinting around the necks of some Danforth supporters to sparkle. The music was louder here, but still a lovely accompaniment to the conversations. A few elegantly dressed couples swirled around the dance floor but most of the guests were clustered around the small tables and chairs set up along the perimeter of the room. Nerves fluttered wildly in the pit of her stomach, but Kim silently ordered them to calm. She'd had years to perfect that ability.

"Do you know all these people?" Zack asked, astonished.

"No. Just a few." Nodding her head, she said, "The tall guy there in the navy blue suit, with his arm around the short woman with the great hair? That's my brother Reid and his fiancée, Tina."

"Uh-huh."

"Beside him," she continued, "are Ian, Adam and Marcus, my other brothers."

"Big family."

"That's not even counting cousins," she said, then grinned. "Like Jacob, there on the dance floor."

She pointed out a tall man with short black hair dusted with gray. He was laughing and spinning a much shorter woman in a wild version of a jitterbug in the middle of the ballroom.

"He looks like he's having fun," Zack said.

"Jacob has fun anywhere," Kim said on a sigh that was only slightly envious.

"So what do we do first?" Zack took her hand and threaded it through the crook of his arm.

"Find my father, I suppose," she said, her gaze already raking the crowd for one face in particular.

She found Abraham Danforth on the far side of the ballroom, deep in discussion with three other men. He didn't look happy. Kim felt a quick jab of anxiety. If Abraham Danforth wasn't smiling at a fund-raiser, there was a problem.

Kim led the way, but kept her hand on Zack's arm. It felt good to have all that barely contained muscle and steel beneath her palm. It made her feel invincible. Almost.

As they approached her father, his voice, lowered to a mere rumble, reached her despite his efforts to keep quiet.

"I don't care what they said, I won't have it," Abraham muttered, his gaze narrowed on the tallest of the three men in black suits.

Kim didn't recognize any of them, but that didn't mean anything. There were always plenty of strangers at these events. But she did spot a flicker of annoyance in the black eyes of the man her father was focused on.

"I assure you—" the man said, his voice colored by an accent she couldn't quite place. Spanish?

A tall, robust man with silvering black hair and sharp eyes that rarely missed anything, Abraham Danforth was not a man to be taken lightly. And judging by the flash of surprise in the black eyes watching her father, Kim thought Abraham's opponent was just realizing that.

"No," Abraham said sharply, cutting the man off midsentence. Moving in closer, Kim's father narrowed his gaze on the man in question and lowered his voice even further. "No one threatens my family, is that understood? If my son Ian has any more trouble, I'm going to take it very personally. Are we clear?"

The other man's mouth tightened into a grim slash across his darkly handsome face. *"Sí."*

Before Kim could wonder what was going on, Zack muttered, "Stay here," and stepped up beside her father. "Anything I can help you with, sir?" he offered, sliding a warning glance to all three men.

Abraham shot Zack a quick, approving glance, then looked back at the other man. "Thank you, but no. I think we're finished here, aren't we, *se-ñor?*"

A short nod was his only answer.

"Fine. Thank you for coming, sorry you have to leave so early." Abraham lifted his left hand, crooked a finger and almost instantly, two equally grim-faced men stepped up to his side. "Show these men out, please."

"Yes sir, Mr. Danforth," one of them said, then turned to the visibly fuming dark-eyed man. "This way, sir."

Kim stepped up to her father's side. "Dad? What's going on?"

A heartbeat or two of thick silence passed before Abraham's features cleared, like storm clouds lifting to reveal a sunny day. "Kim, honey. Don't you look lovely?" He turned and held out one hand to Zack. "And you must be Zack Sheridan. You look just like your father did twenty years ago. Great to meet you."

"Dad," Kim said again, tugging at her father's coat sleeve. "Never mind introductions. What's going on?"

"Nothing for you to worry about," he insisted, before beaming at Zack again. "Thanks for your offer of help."

"Not a problem," Zack said, letting his gaze slide briefly to Kim's furious eyes. "SEALs stick together."

Abraham sighed and smiled. "My SEAL days were long ago, I'm afraid."

"Once a SEAL," Zack said, "always a SEAL."

Abraham grinned. "Hoo-yah, Commander Sheridan."

"Exactly."

"If you two have finished your bonding dance," Kim said, her voice low enough, tight enough, to demand their attention, "I wonder if you might spare me a moment for the 'womenfolk'?"

Her father frowned slightly, then shook his head. "No more unpleasantness tonight, Kimberly. It's your brother's big night."

She sighed. "Dad, Reid doesn't know half these people."

"It's still his engagement party. Let's not forget that, hmm?"

"But what about Ian?"

He frowned again, deeper this time. "Please keep your voice down. There was a threat made. Some Colombian drug lord was rattling his saber. I've taken care of it."

"Drug lords?" she repeated, eyes wide.

"Shh." Clearly exasperated, he grabbed Zack's arm and said, "Commander, dance with my daughter."

"A pleasure, sir," Zack said and took Kim's hand, closing his fingers around hers when she would have escaped. "Come on," he whispered, leading her onto the dance floor. "No point in fighting a battle you're not going to win."

Still fuming, she tossed a look back at her father. "What kind of thing is that for a SEAL to say?"

He swung her into his arms, pulling her tightly against him. Smiling down into her grass-green eyes, he shrugged and said, "Honey, you're no SEAL, so give it up. Your old man doesn't want to talk about it and you're not going to change his mind."

"But—"

"Always a 'but' with you," he said, smiling, and swayed to the rhythm of the music soaring through the huge room. "Just for once, let that go and just dance with me."

She opened her mouth as if to argue, then, still staring up at him, deliberately snapped it shut again.

"That cost you, didn't it?" His whisper was for her alone.

"More than you know," she admitted, sliding her left hand up to his shoulder as she moved in time with his steps.

"Well then, here's something to take your mind off it."

"What?"

"You're beautiful."

She blinked up at him.

"Remember," he said, seeing the doubt flash in her eyes, "I don't lie."

She nodded slowly, keeping her gaze locked with his. "Thank you."

"You're welcome." Around them, couples moved in time to the music and conversations were being carried on from the sidelines. Deals were being made, promises crafted and lies exchanged. But here, with Kim in his arms, Zack felt as though they were alone on the planet. It was just the two of them, locked together.

He felt her breath shudder from her lungs. Felt the solid beat of her heart against his chest and the pure pleasure of her thighs brushing along his.

The short, black dress she wore fit her like a lover's caress. It hugged her curves and defined every tidy inch of her. The high heels on her small feet did amazing things for her legs. Her long, midnight-black hair was braided close to her skull, then fell in a long straight rope to the middle of her back. All he could think of while the end of that soft rope brushed over his hand was undoing the braid, threading his fingers through the mass of hair and pulling it all over him like a cool, black curtain.

Mouth dry, heart pounding, he somehow kept moving, swaying to the music that seemed to be pumping inside him. When she laid her cheek on his shoulder, he inhaled the soft, flowery scent of her hair and knew he was a dead man.

Everything about this woman called out to him on so many levels. He wanted her. Wanted to be inside her. Wanted to hold her and be held.

And he didn't think he'd be able to wait for her to come to him.

Zack reluctantly gave way as an older gentleman cut in and spun Kim into a waltz. She smiled at him over her new partner's shoulder and Zack held on to that smile while the next hour crawled by.

He mingled, feeling uncomfortable and wondering what the hell he was doing at this kind of a party. The whole place reeked of money and it hit Zack hard to realize that Kim was used to all of this. That she'd grown up in circumstances he would never be able to relate to. They were from such widely different backgrounds, they could have been from two different planets.

And yet, he couldn't keep his gaze off her.

She moved through the crowd with an ease and grace he admired all the more because he could see the discomfort in her eyes. No one else did, though, and he was proud of her. She handled strangers and friends alike. Always a warm smile and a few kind words. Zack stayed on the periphery of the party, where he could watch and still keep to himself. And his view of Kim kept his blood pumping. He couldn't seem to quell the rush of his blood when she was near. Couldn't seem to stop the desire that pumped through him every time he looked at her.

So he quit trying.

He listened to speeches, and even paid attention when Abraham, reacting to a request from a guest, retold the story of Miss Carlisle, the Danforth ghost. Comforting to know he wasn't the only one who'd been surprised with a visit from the dead.

But after an hour or more of smiling and fielding stupid questions about the military, Zack was near the end of both his rope and his patience. Sidling onto the dance floor, he stole Kim from the arms of yet another old Southern gentleman and quickly whirled her to a corner of the room. His hand slid up and down her spine and she smiled up at him.

"Having fun?"

"Oh, yeah," he said wryly, pulling her more tightly to him. "Haven't had this much fun since the last time our chopper went down in the desert."

One corner of her mouth tipped up. "If it makes you feel any better, my feet are killing me."

He glanced at the pointy-toed heels. "They may not be comfortable, but they look great."

"Small consolation."

"Not from where I'm standing."

"Are you always this smooth?"

Zack grinned. The whole damn party was tolerable now that he had her in his arms again. "Do you really have to ask?"

"I'm glad you're here, even if you're having a lousy time," she said.

"Right now, I'd have to say I'm enjoying myself."

"Me, too," Kim admitted and swayed with him as he kept time with the music.

She slid her hand higher up on his shoulder and leaned into him. Zack tightened his grip on her right hand and tucked it next to his chest. "You know, Doc," he said, "I was thinking we could—"

"Kimberly, is that you?" A deep voice cut him off neatly.

Scowling, Zack shot a glance at the man who'd interrupted them. But when Kim stiffened in his arms, his protective instincts went on full alert.

She pulled away from him slightly and might have stepped out of his arms, had he allowed it. But Zack kept her pressed close to him even as she turned to look at the couple who'd stopped alongside them.

The shorter man had thick blond hair and small blue eyes. His smile was picture-perfect, but Zack thought his chin looked weak. The woman beside him was a stunner, from her dark red hair to the tips of her bloodred polished toes. A beauty, Zack thought, but a little cold around the eyes.

"Hello, Charles," Kim said.

Ah, Zack thought. The idiot.

"You're looking...well," Charles said, "isn't she, Elizabeth?"

His wife, though, hardly glanced at Kim. Instead her gaze locked on to Zack as she asked, "And you are?"

"Grateful," Zack said, tightening his grip on Kim and sliding one hand down her spine in an intimate caress that couldn't be missed.

"I'm sorry?" Charles said.

"Yes, you are, aren't you, Chuck?" Zack said.

A stunned silence ticked past.

"Charles, Elizabeth," Kim said, speaking up to fill the void, "this is Zack Sheridan."

"I'm glad we got a chance to meet, Chuck," Zack said, deliberately using the name that had the other man flinching. He ran one hand idly up and down Kim's arm in a proprietary gesture the other man didn't miss. "Wanted to thank you for being such an ass."

Charles's eyes popped in insulted surprise. "I beg your pardon?"

"No need," Zack assured him, fighting down the urge to plow a fist into that weak chin. This was the man who'd hurt Kim? Hell, he wasn't even worth hitting. He'd go down too easy. "You're forgiven."

"I don't—"

"Zack," Kim said, glancing at the other dancers as if afraid someone might overhear.

But Zack kept his voice pitched at a level directed solely at Barrington. "After all," he said, as if Kim hadn't interrupted him, "if you hadn't been such a chump, I wouldn't be here with Kim. So thanks again. Now, good night."

With that, he swung Kim into a wide circle and kept them moving until they were on the far side of the floor.

"I can't believe you just did that," she said, staring up at him, a smile dazzling her eyes and tugging at her mouth.

"I can't believe you're surprised," he quipped.

"Me, either," she said with a laugh that made him feel as though someone had just pinned a medal on his chest. "Thanks."

His hand swept up and down her spine again and he watched as flames of desire lit up her eyes. "Trust me on this," he said. "My pleasure."

"Zack…"

"How long do we have to stay at this thing?" His voice was low and tight, aching with a need that was suddenly so sharp, so vicious, it clawed at him.

"I don't—"

"I need you, Kim," he said, forcing the words past the knot in his throat that threatened to suffocate him on the spot. "I can't wait for you to come to me." He tightened his arm around her waist, pulling her flush against him until she was bound to feel the thick, hard proof of his desires pushing at her.

Her eyes slid closed and a whisper of air slipped through her lips. "Zack, I…"

"I admit it, Kim. I want you." His gaze moved over her face and his heart pumped furiously. "I want you so bad, I may not be able to walk out of here."

She lifted her gaze to his and stared hard at him for a long moment. Then she licked her lips, inhaled sharply and said, "Can you run?"

Nine

Zack kept his foot on the accelerator and took every red light like a personal insult.

Jaw clenched, gaze narrowed on the road in front of him, Zack fought down the urge to pull the car over to the curb and just have her right there. It was all he could do to keep his hands on the wheel—when he wanted them on her. He'd never wanted anything in his life the way he wanted Kim Danforth. Her perfume filled his head. Heat from her body reached out for him across the bucket seats and seemed to singe him, even with the open space separating them. Every short, strangled breath she drew rattled through him, leaving him just a little more shaken than he'd been before.

His heart hammering in his chest, Zack told himself it was ridiculous, that he was acting like a teenager about to get lucky with a cheerleader.

It didn't seem to matter.

His blood raced in time with the SUV as it swerved in and out of traffic. He heard Kim gasp when he took a corner a little more sharply than he'd planned. "Sorry, sorry," he muttered. "I'll slow down."

"Don't you dare," she whispered tightly and those three words were enough to have him floor the gas pedal and pray for green lights.

"Right. No slowing down."

The Danforth mansion was far behind them now. The crowds, the music, the inane chatter that had swelled to the ceiling, trapping them both for far too long in polite society—it was all gone. Now, it was just the two of them and nothing else mattered. It was as if the desire that had crouched between them so hungrily had suddenly erupted, tearing at them both with vicious tugs and pulls that couldn't be denied any longer.

Zack didn't even care that he had been the one to break first. Didn't mind that she hadn't come to him. All he cared about now was having his hands on her. His mind filled with images, one after the other. Visions of them tangled together on her bed. His hands sliding up her long, sleek legs, fisting in her hair. His mouth on hers as he entered her.

He groaned tightly and ordered his brain to shut down. All he needed was to wrap the damn car around a telephone pole. If he died in a wreck before he'd had a chance to bed Kim, he'd be one pissed-off ghost.

Taking the right turn onto her street, Zack emptied his mind of everything but parking the damn car. He pulled into the driveway, threw the car into Park, yanked up the brake, turned the engine off and reached for Kim.

She was on the same page.

Unlatching her seat belt, she leaned into him, moving into his embrace as if the only thing that had been holding her back was the canvas strap.

Zack pulled her across the gap between the seats and pinned her on his lap. She scooted around until she was comfortable, grinding her hips and bottom against his already hard, tight body.

"Doc," he murmured, between brief, hot tastes of her mouth, "you're killin' me here."

"No," she said, sliding her hands up to cup his face, "not yet. I want you alive and well and...I just want you."

"Good, babe, that's good." He took her mouth completely this time, giving in to the need to taste her. To feel her sighs slide into him, to feel the warmth of her.

He savored her, drinking her in and giving himself the pleasure of this first discovery. This wonder of mouths and tongues and breaths, mingling, blending, becoming one. And he felt the slam of something powerful punch at him as he held her tighter, closer, pressing her body against his until he felt her hardened nipples pushing into his chest like tiny firebrands.

Zack slid one hand up her thigh, under the hem of that short black dress and groaned when he found the tops of her sheer black thigh-high stockings—a wide, elastic band of lace. Instantly, his mind filled with the picture of Kim, wearing only those stockings and the roaring in his ears told him his blood was pumping wild and hot.

She shifted in his grasp, sliding around on his lap again as his fingers drifted higher, higher.

"Zack…"

"Just let me touch you, darlin'," he murmured, bending his head to kiss her neck, nibbling at her flesh with lips and teeth.

"Oh, boy," she whispered, tipping her head to one side, giving him easier access.

"Oh, yeah," he said, his breath dusting her skin. She was all. She was everything. She fit in his arms as though made for him. The way she turned into his chest, the way she curled her arms around his neck and pressed her lips to his throat—she was so much more than he'd ever found before. So much more than he'd expected or hoped for.

Outside the car, Kim's neighborhood was dark

and silent. Homes were locked up for the night and the only sound other than their own breathing was that of a dog, somewhere in the distance, howling at the moon. Zack knew just how the mutt felt. Hell, he wanted to howl, too.

He slid his fingers higher up her thigh, close, so close to the center of her heat.

She lifted her hips and her head fell back as she gasped, a quick, sharp intake of breath. "Zack, I want—"

"Me, too, darlin'," he said, lowering his head to kiss the base of her throat. "I can't wait. I have to touch you now."

She lifted her head to look at him, and in the wash of moonlight, her eyes looked impossibly dark and full of secrets. Their gazes locked and she cupped his face in her palms. "I don't want to wait another minute, Zack," she said softly, each word hitting him like a velvet bullet, slamming into his chest, his mind, his heart. "Touch me, Zack," she whispered, leaning close for a kiss. "Touch me now."

Her mouth came down on his as his hand moved to cup her heat. She moaned and shifted uncomfortably, but he held her still. A man on a mission now, he swept his hand up her thigh, grabbed the edge of what felt like lace panties and gave them a quick twist. They tore easily and just like that, he had his hands on her.

In her.

She sucked in a gulp of air and kissed him again, hungrily, mating her tongue to his, and Zack's heart thundered in a heavy rhythm that rattled his ears and shook him to his bones. Lifting her hips for him, she groaned from the back of her throat as he pushed first one finger, then two, into her damp, waiting heat.

He tore his mouth from hers and breathed like a man coming up from twenty fathoms. She arched in his grasp and her legs fell apart, wider, wider, offering him more, offering him everything. He took. His thumb dusted the small nub of flesh at the heart of her and she cried out, her voice breaking on his name.

"Zack, it's too much, it's too—"

"Not enough, babe," he whispered, his own voice cracking on the hard knot of lust lodged in his throat. "Not nearly enough." His fingers dipped in and out of her heat, pushing her, driving her, higher and higher. Her hips pumped, her breath quickened and danced in and out of her lungs on a frantic beat.

"Feels good. Feels…" She stiffened, and a low, keening moan slid from her throat as her body dissolved into a starburst of sensation.

"Right," he murmured, staring into her eyes as the first explosion ripped through her body. "It feels right."

* * *

Heart pounding, throat tight, Kim felt every cell in her body go soft and gooey and slide into a near-liquid state. If he hadn't been holding on to her, she probably would have *oozed* off his lap and onto the floor of the car.

The car.

Oh, boy. She'd just had the best orgasm of her life in the front seat of a car parked in her drive-way.

Her brain whispered that she should be ashamed of herself.

Her body told her brain to shut up and enjoy the ride.

''That was,'' she said as soon as she thought she could speak without whimpering, ''amazing.''

''Wait until I have more room to maneuver,'' he said, one corner of his mouth tipping into a smile that tugged at her heart.

''Wow.''

''That about covers it,'' he agreed and smoothed the hem of her skirt down her thighs. ''Now how about we get inside and finish what we started?''

''You bet,'' Kim said, eager now for more. Her body still humming from his touch, she wanted more. Needed more. Needed to feel him filling her, his body sliding into hers, pushing her up that glo-rious peak one more time.

He opened the car door and stepped out, carrying her with him.

"I can walk," she said.

"And I can carry you," he told her, bending his head for a brief, hard kiss. "I like this way better."

Her, too, Kim thought. She felt like the heroine in a romantic movie. The handsome naval officer sweeping her off her feet and carrying her off for a long night of lovemaking.

How, she wondered, had this happened to her life? How had she gone from being a lonely marine biologist to having a sexual experience in a parked car, in less than two weeks? And how could she ever go back to the way her life was before Zack had entered it?

He stepped up onto the porch and promptly slung her over his left shoulder as he dug for his keys.

"Hey!" She pushed herself up by planting her hands on his back. "This is slightly less romantic, Sheridan."

He unlocked the door, then reached up to smooth the palm of his hand across her bare bottom. His fingers kneaded her soft flesh, sparking new needs, new desires. Kim shivered at the intimate caress and nearly melted against him.

"Give me a chance, Doc," he said as he carried her into the tiny house, "I'm just getting started."

"Promises, promises." She swung the door

closed behind them and Zack headed straight for her bedroom.

He walked through the open doorway and stepped up alongside the bed. Then with one smooth flip, he had her on her back on the mattress, staring up at him as he tore at his uniform blouse.

"Peaches, you want romantic, you've got it." He grinned as he got rid of his clothing in record time. Then he was naked, standing in front of her and all Kim could do was stare.

She couldn't take her eyes off him. Moonlight speared through the bedroom window and shone on him, defining every muscle, every hard edge and scar. He took her breath away. His eyes gleamed as he watched her and Kim's stomach jumped when desire flashed across his eyes.

"Now you, darlin'," he said.

Nodding, Kim scooted to the edge of the bed. Then she turned around and said, "Unzip me?" She could have done it herself, but she wanted his hands on her. She wanted to feel the whisper-soft touch of his fingers along her spine.

The zipper pulled free with a sigh of sound and his hands followed it down, smoothing along her back, curving along her hips.

"No bra," he said, turning her in his arms as he pushed the fabric of her dress down, letting it fall to the floor in a chic black puddle.

''No,'' she said and hissed in a breath as his hands cupped her breasts, his thumbs and forefingers tweaking her already rigid nipples into hard buds of aching need. ''You have magic hands,'' she whispered.

He chuckled. ''You ain't seen nothin' yet.''

Kim swayed into him, then bent slightly to tug her thigh-high black stockings off. He caught her hands in his and shook his head.

''The stockings stay.''

A curl of something wicked and delicious unwound in the pit of Kim's stomach. ''Yeah?''

''Oh, yeah,'' he said, his gaze dropping to sweep over her with a long, approving look. ''Babe, you are a fantasy.''

''I'm real enough,'' she said, lifting her hands to encircle his neck.

He stared at her and Kim tried to read the emotions dazzling across the surface of his eyes, but they came and went so quickly, she couldn't be sure of any of them. All she knew was that she felt good in his arms. She felt beautiful and sexy and wild and free.

She'd never been any of those things and knowing that she could be, with Zack, was so liberating, she could hardly catch her breath.

''Lie down,'' he said softly, tipping her back onto the mattress. ''Now you get your romance.''

"Be inside me, Zack," she said. "I want to feel you deep inside me."

His jaw clenched and he inhaled sharply. "Me, too, but first I want to kiss every inch of your body."

She shivered and lost herself in the dark gleam of his eyes. "Zack…"

"Trust me."

"I do."

He smiled and leaned over her. He started at the base of her throat, trailing damp, hot kisses down to her breasts. Then he took her nipples, first one, then the other, into his mouth. He suckled her, drawing and pulling at her sensitive flesh until Kim could hardly be still. She writhed beneath him, twisting with the building fires within. His breath caressed her skin and fanned the flames until she thought she might spontaneously combust. She didn't really care, as long as he kept doing what he was doing.

He moved, nibbling his way down her stomach, across her abdomen and to the juncture of her thighs. Kim stiffened and inched back instinctively. But Zack's strong hands grabbed her hips and held her in place. She looked down at him as he knelt between her thighs and she managed to say, "Zack, you don't have to—"

"I said every inch, babe." He smiled, winked

and lowered his head to take her in the most intimate kiss she'd ever experienced.

Kim sighed and she was pretty sure she whined a little, too. It was just so perfect. So wonderful. So wicked. His tongue moved over her most tender flesh and she arched wildly, moving into him as he took her higher than she'd ever been before. His breath puffed against her, his lips and tongue and teeth tortured her with a sweet relentlessness that pushed her ever closer to the edge of madness.

And when the first tremors shook through her, he tasted her surrender, holding her gently, lovingly, until she drifted back to earth, still in the cradle of his strong hands.

Head still swimming, Kim looked at him and watched as he sheathed himself before covering her body with his.

"You make a hell of a picture, darlin'," he said, "wearing nothing but moonlight and those stockings."

"You make a hell of a picture yourself," Kim said, smiling as her blood sizzled and popped, "wearing nothing at all."

"All I want to be wearing is you," he murmured, dropping a quick, hard kiss on her mouth.

"Be in me," she said, cupping his face between her palms. "I want to feel you, Zack. I want to feel you inside."

"Now," he agreed and pushed his way home.

Kim gasped and arched into him, lifting her legs to lock around his hips. She pulled him tighter, closer, wanting to feel as much of him as she could. His hips rocked as he buried his face in the curve of her neck. She felt the rhythm quicken, felt her blood do a dance of welcome and her heart sing. He filled her. Completely. Totally. He pushed himself high enough inside her that she thought he actually touched her heart.

Kim lifted her arms to hold him to her and she relished the pounding of his heart against her chest. He lifted his head to look down at her and as their eyes met, that slow rush to completion flashed between them. Kim felt it first, then saw the same explosive shudders lance across Zack's eyes.

And this time when she fell, he was right there, taking the fall with her.

Ten

Zack knew he should move. Unfortunately, he'd forgotten how.

Every muscle in his body was lax. Yet at the same time, he felt energized. His blood rushed through his veins, his heart raced in a wild, frantic beat and his mind was busily trying to find a way to explain what had just happened.

But explanations weren't easy.

It wasn't just sex.

What he and Kim had shared went way above and beyond the simple easing of need. If it had been only lust, the urges in him would have been satisfied. He could have gotten out of bed, dressed and walked away—as he had so many times before.

But now, for the first time, he wanted to stay. That thought alone was usually enough to have him rolling away from her. Putting both emotional and physical distance between them. He stared blankly at the ceiling like a shell-shocked survivor of a fiercely pitched battle.

Beside him, Kim yawned, stretched languidly and sighed as she slid one foot along his leg. New need zapped him, sizzling along his veins like an out-of-control skyrocket. Then she pushed her hair back from her face and said softly, "That was..."

"Yeah," he said, congratulating himself on being able to talk. "That about covers it."

She turned into him, curling her body along his, burrowing her head into the curve of his shoulder. His skin tingled, as if lit from within by thousands of sparklers. The scent of her hair reached him and enveloped him completely. Would he ever again be able to notice the smell of flowers without thinking of her? Of this moment?

She ran the flat of her hand across his chest and fires quickened inside him. Moments before, he'd been sated, now, new hunger rose inside him again, demanding satisfaction. He'd never felt this before. This all-encompassing need for one particular woman.

And a part of him pulled back from that acknowledgement.

Zack closed his eyes and captured her hand in his, holding her still, hoping it would be enough to rein in the desire pumping afresh through his body.

"I have to say," Kim said softly, her voice a low hush in the moonlit room, "I've never enjoyed the end of a party so much."

"I aim to please." His voice was light, his words casual, in an attempt to convince them both that what had just happened wasn't as mind-boggling as he seemed to think it was. But whatever he said, it wouldn't be enough to chase away the stray thoughts still bulleting around his brain.

Several long moments passed in silence and Zack's mind took that quiet and ran with it. Image after image filled his mind and they were all of Kim. Kim laughing, Kim walking along the river, the wind in her hair. Kim tonight, surrounded by her family and the immense wealth she'd grown up with.

That image stung.

He couldn't stop the sudden doubt. He'd grown up in a solid, middle-class family, the only child of hardworking people who'd lived the same kind of military life he now led. Their family had been small, but tight. Right now, his parents were off in an RV, discovering the country, and Zack was pretty much on his own. The navy was his family. His team members his brothers. That had been enough for him.

Until recently, his mind taunted.

He'd built a life he loved. One that didn't lend itself well to sharing. Zack scowled up at the ceiling. He'd tried once before, hadn't he? But his lack of a fortune—and the fact that he didn't give a good damn about making pots of money—had ended that before it could begin.

So, he thought now, if he hadn't been enough for *her,* how could he possibly think that he would be enough for Kim Danforth? She hadn't been born with just a silver spoon in her mouth; it had been the whole silverware set.

People with that kind of money simply weren't interested in anyone outside their own realm.

Not that he cared or anything.

Not that he'd been thinking of doing anything so crazy as proposing.

Not that he was in love.

Oh, man.

He scraped one hand across his face, hoping to wipe away the thoughts crowding his mind. But it didn't help. Nothing could.

He was in deep and he knew it.

"What're you thinking?"

"Hmm?" Kim's voice had startled him out of his train wreck of a thought process. For which, he told himself, he was grateful. Quickly, he searched for something to say. "I was uh, remembering that little speech your father gave."

She laughed a little, her breath dusting across his chest like a whisper. "Which one?"

"The one about the ghost."

"Poor Miss Carlisle." She shook her head and her hair shifted like warm silk against his skin. "Imagine arriving for a job as governess, only to be run down on the drive before you could reach the front door."

Ghosts. A safe topic, he thought.

"You'd think she'd quit trying to get in," he said. "After a hundred years or so of attempts."

"She's determined to make it into the house," Kim said softly. "Almost as determined as I was to get out of it."

She'd made it, he thought. Out of that house and into this bungalow that seemed light years away from the mansion they'd visited hours ago. She'd made her own life, apart from the Danforths. She'd carved out a world of her own. But that didn't mean that she wasn't still a part of that influential family.

"Some things," he told her, his voice thoughtful, "just aren't meant to be."

"You believe that?" She tipped her head back to look up at him.

Zack met her gaze and tried, this time, not to

notice just how green her eyes were. Just how hypnotic it was to stare into those depths and feel them draw you deeper, closer. And somehow, he knew that he'd be seeing those eyes of hers in his dreams for the rest of his life. She'd branded him somehow, and even when he left her—as he knew he would—he'd never really be free of her.

Zack held her closer and with his other hand, smoothed her hair back from her face, letting his fingertips glide along her cheek. The smooth slide of flesh against flesh warmed him, comforted him. "Sometimes," he said, "it's better to walk away."

"I don't believe that."

"I never used to," he admitted and wondered if she realized that he was already pulling back. He wouldn't admit to what he was feeling for her because there would be no point. There was no future for them.

"But now you do?" She went up on one elbow and looked down at him.

"Now," he said, staring up at her and feeling the raw pulse of need reach up and grab him by the throat. "Now I don't know what I believe."

"Do you know what you want?"

His mouth lifted in a brief twist of a smile even as a cold, unseen hand squeezed his heart until his chest ached. "At the moment...you."

She lowered her head to his, her thick, black hair hanging like a curtain of midnight silk on either side of them. "Then for now, let the wanting be enough."

"Doc," he said, already reaching for her, "I like the way you think."

He closed his mind to thoughts of tomorrow. To the warnings his brain tried to send. Because all he cared about right now was Kim's warm flesh pressed to his. The shine in her eyes and the curve of her mouth.

Zack had seen enough in his life to know that it was important to enjoy what you had while you had it, to appreciate the moment because that moment might not come again.

He scooped her up, pulled her on top of him, then wrapped his arms around her, pinning her to him. Their bodies brushed together, length to length, hard to soft. His hands skimmed up her spine, defining every line, every curve, his fingers exploring, carving the feel of her into his memory. He wanted Kim so deeply in his heart, his mind, that she was always there, just a thought away. Zack knew that in some distant future, the memories of this night, this moment, might be all he had left to remind him that once he'd held a woman who was everything to him.

She kissed him, her mouth on his aroused him so fiercely, he devoured her in response. Taking her head in his hands, he held her mouth fused to his, taking, demanding what she offered and giving all that he had to give. She sighed and he felt the ripple of it course down to his soul. Her breath became his. Their hearts beat in tandem. Blood raced and pulses skipped.

He wanted her as he had no other. But more, he needed her as he'd never expected to need anyone.

Rolling to one side, he tipped her onto her back and indulged himself by caressing her body in long, slow strokes. She damn near purred as she arched into him, digging her head back into the pillow, fanning that black silk hair beneath her.

This was good, he thought, dipping his head to taste first one of her breasts and then the next. She groaned and the flames within him licked at the corners of his heart. This was right, he thought, trailing kisses up the column of her throat and across her jaw before reaching her mouth. This was all, he thought, as once again, he tasted her, invading her warmth, letting himself slide into the heat and magic that was Kim.

"Zack," she whispered, her breath warm on his face. "If we keep this up, we're going to kill ourselves."

"Hell of a way to go though, peaches," he said, taking another kiss, then one more.

"Yes," she said on a sigh of wonder, "yes, it is."

Her hands skimmed up his back and he felt the strength in them. Short, neat nails scraped at his flesh and he felt the stroke of each one as if she were carving her initials into his heart. Marking him as hers.

That thought drove him, plunging through his mind like a runaway train. Need swept through him like a tidal wave, relentless, unavoidable, devastating.

Zack rode the crest of that wave and moved over her, sliding up the length of her. He watched the flash of desire snap across the surface of her eyes. Felt her desperation as she grabbed him, held him, lifting her hips in a silent, ancient welcome. And giving himself up to the flames within, he entered her again, claimed her again, and in the act of completion, found more need.

He linked his fingers with hers, needing that extra connection. He stared down into her eyes, and saw himself mirrored there. He watched her watch him and gazes locked, they reached the shattering end that somehow signaled a beginning.

The days marched past, one after the other, measured in sunrise and sunset. The hours in between were filled with sex and laughter and a freedom that Kim had never known before.

In Zack, she'd found a man who understood her love of the sea. A man who was more than willing to spend an hour or two scuba diving on the off chance they might see something spectacular.

Around Zack, she didn't feel like the nerd she'd always been. She felt…beautiful. And smart. And interesting.

And most importantly, at least to her, she felt…wanted.

He touched her and her skin sizzled. He looked at her and her blood raced. He kissed her and she melted. Since the night of the party, they'd been together. Every night, he came to her bed and in the morning, he was still there. Her heart was entwined with his, her life felt fuller and richer with him in it. And she wasn't at all sure what she would do when he left.

She'd accepted long ago that she wasn't going to find that one man. That she wouldn't have the family, the children, she'd dreamed of having when she was a girl. After that mess with Charles, she'd simply acknowledged to herself that she wasn't the kind of woman men fell in love with. She was, as she'd always been, too smart, too practical, too uninterested in the things other women seemed fascinated by.

She'd much rather spend the day underwater, charting fish, than spend hours wandering through a crowded mall searching for just the right outfit to wear to a society luncheon. She was happier keeping her long hair in a braid rather than face the nightmare of regular visits to a salon. She didn't enjoy small talk, and she'd rather have her fingernails torn out than be forced to sit through terminally boring board meetings.

There was a price to be paid for living the kind of life she preferred, and she'd long ago come to grips with the fact that her price would be solitude.

And then Zack Sheridan had marched into her nice, neat, solitary world and splintered it.

Sitting at the kitchen table, surrounded by her books and the paper she was supposed to be working on, Kim glanced over at the tall crystal vase that held what was left of her first Valentine bouquet. A week ago, Zack had brought her two dozen yellow roses, a box of truffles and, she thought with a smile, a new valve for the oxygen tank she used on her dives.

What woman wouldn't fall in love with a man like that?

''Love?'' She whispered the word as though afraid that Zack would hear her. But he was outside in the backyard, mowing her tiny patch of grass. Pushing up from the table, she tossed her pen onto an open book and watched as it rolled right off the table. *Love?*

Her breath huffed in and out of her lungs. Her head took a wild spin that had the room tilting for one brief, fascinating moment and she was almost positive her heart had lurched to a stop.

She was in love.

Really in love, for the first and last time in her life.

"I should have seen this coming," she said, still half-stunned by her own discovery. "But even if I had," she reasoned, starting to pace now while her thoughts raced to keep up, "how could I have stopped it?" More importantly, "Why would I have?"

Well, because, you idiot, she told herself silently, life would be a lot less complicated if you hadn't let your heart get involved.

"But complicated can be good." She stopped pacing. "Can't it?"

Sunlight poured through the front windows and painted gold slashes across her furniture and the polished wood floor. From outside came the sound of the hand mower in the backyard, Zack's colorful cursing and, just beneath those homey sounds, the quiet music of the wind chimes hanging from the roof of the house. Kids skateboarded along the sidewalk, the wheels on their boards growling like caged beasts let loose for a much needed run.

The world was just the same as it had been ten minutes ago. And yet, she thought, wandering down the hall to the back door where she could stand and watch Zack, it was all so different.

He'd taken his shirt off as he worked on the yard and in the direct sunlight, his tanned muscles gleamed with sweat. The scars marking his body stood out a bit paler than the rest of his flesh, but somehow made him look *more* perfect rather than less so. Sunglasses shielded his eyes and a day's growth of whiskers dotted his face. His large, strong hands gripped the handles of the ancient mower and something inside Kim *pinged* in appreciation as she watched him tighten that grip.

What was she supposed to do about this, she wondered. How could she keep loving him to herself? But how could she tell him when she knew he was only here because it was his duty to protect her? They'd said nothing about tomorrow. They'd made no plans for anything beyond the month that was nearly up.

She laid one hand on the cool glass of the window half of the door, and watched, smiling, as he cursed the mower that continued to fight him. Her heart turned over and Kim knew that she had to do something.

She couldn't simply stand by and watch him walk out of her life as easily as he'd walked into it.

After dinner, when the phone rang, Zack reached for it first. Hell, he'd lunged for the phone as if it were the last lifeline in a churning sea.

He'd tried to keep busy. Tried to stay so wrapped up in one project or another that his mind wouldn't have time to torture him with thoughts of leaving Kim. But it seemed that no matter how busy he was, his brain was free to wander. And it did. Constantly.

Their month was nearly over, and soon he'd be shipping out again. Though a part of him knew that was a good thing, another, more hungry part of him dreaded it as he had never dreaded anything.

His career had been built around deployment. One mission fed into the next and he'd always liked it that way. New people, new countries, new problems to solve. New dangers and adventures. Him and his team.

But things were changing.

Three Card had a wife, for God's sake.

Hunter was still laid up in the hospital.

And Zack had found Kim.

''Yeah?'' He damn near growled into the phone. An instant later, a chill swept over him as he listened to Kim's brother Ian tell him about the latest threat delivered to their father.

When Kim came up beside him, he reached out and took her hand. Feeling the chill in her skin, he folded his fingers around hers, trying not to notice how fragile her hand felt in his.

''What is it?'' she whispered.

''Any leads?'' he asked Kim's brother Ian, ignoring her.

''Nothing,'' Ian said. ''Just the words, 'I'm still watching you,' signed by Lady Savannah.''

"The woman needs a new routine."

"The woman needs to be locked up," Ian countered, his voice tight.

"I'm with you there," Zack said, letting go of Kim long enough to drape one arm around her shoulder and pull her in close.

Ian continued a moment later. "The cops think they've got a lead, so just keep an eye on my little sister, huh?"

"Don't worry about her," Zack said. "I'll take care of her." Until the navy pulled him away, his brain screamed. And then what? Who would look out for her then? Who would be with her when he was off halfway around the world doing God knew what?

Mind seething, he hung up, setting the phone receiver back into its cradle much more gently than he wanted to.

"It's my father again, isn't it?" Kim asked.

"Yeah," he said, turning to her, pulling her close to him. "Another threat."

"When is this going to stop?"

"Ian says they have leads."

"I hope so," she said, tipping her head back to look up at him.

"You're safe with me." Zack stared down into her green eyes and felt that magnetic pull working on him again. He smoothed her hair back, letting the thick, soft strands sift between his fingers.

"I know that." She slid her hands beneath the hem of his T-shirt, then wrapped her arms around his middle.

Her touch slammed into him and carried the same force it had the very first time. He wondered if it would always be like that between them, then immediately crushed the thought, since he would never know the answer to that question. Their time was almost up. And when it was, they'd each return to their own worlds, with nothing more than a few damn good memories to cling to.

Cupping her face in his palm, he bent his head for a kiss and when she nibbled at his bottom lip, Zack felt a jolt of desire spear up from deep within him.

Deliberately, he put the world aside and forgot about the threats and leaving her and anything else beyond this one moment.

"I want you again," he whispered, his breath dusting her lips, her cheeks.

"You can have me again," she said, going up on her toes to press her mouth to his. "And again and again and again..."

Zack smiled as he kissed her and felt the first wave of longing rise up to drown him in her magic.

Eleven

Two days later, they were that much closer to the end of the month and no clearer on what would be happening next.

There'd been no more threats made against Kim's father, the man who would be Senator. And as far as Zack was concerned, the actual threat to Kim herself had never been a viable one. The idea of her having a bodyguard, was, as she'd said, more to make her father feel better than because of a real need for protection.

He'd been there nearly a month and he'd seen no real danger to Kim. If anything, she'd proven to be a danger to *him*.

Zack frowned as he listened with half an ear to the rush of water from inside the house. He turned his mind away from imagining Kim in the shower, her long black hair clinging to her wet body. But it wasn't easy. He had some fond memories of that cramped, tiled shower. And those memories were going to have to last him a lifetime.

Neither of them was talking about the end of the month, only a few days away now. They each seemed determined to avoid the subject. And if that was cowardly, well, it was the only damn cowardly thing he'd done in his life, so Zack was willing to live with it.

Beat the hell out of being miserable about something that couldn't be changed.

And for now, at least, he had a distraction. Hula had stopped by and while Kim showered, Zack and his friend took a couple of beers to the backyard.

"You must be ready to get back to the action, huh?"

No. For the first time in more than ten years, no. But he couldn't admit that. Not even to Hula. Zack shot his friend a quick look and lifted one shoulder in a shrug. He took a long sip from the beer bottle, then cupped it in both hands between his up-drawn knees. "You get any word on what's up next?"

"Nothin', man." Hula grinned and winked.

"They don't tell me a damn thing. You're the team leader, brudda."

"Right." Stupid question. Hell, he knew as well as Hula did that none of them would get their next assignment until they'd reported back in for duty. God, even his brain wasn't working anymore.

"So what about the doc?"

"Huh?"

Hula shook his head, reached out and clinked the neck of his beer bottle against Zack's. "Man, you got it bad, don't you?"

"I don't know what you're talking about."

He snorted. "Yeah, I believe you."

"Shut up, Hula."

"I'll shut up, soon as I tell you that you're bein' a damn fool."

Zack scowled at him, even knowing that it wouldn't affect his friend. Hula had stopped fearing Zack's wrath years ago, and fear wasn't about to kick in again now.

"Damn, Shooter," the man said quietly, "that's a hell of a woman."

"You think I don't know that?"

"So, if you love her, tell her."

"Nobody said anything about love," Zack countered tightly. The word had been rocketing around inside him for weeks, but he'd be damned if he'd admit that to Hula if he couldn't get himself to say it to Kim. "Besides, who're you? Advice to the lovelorn?"

"Yeah, that's me. Just ask Three Card."

True enough. Just the summer before, Hula had been the one to give Three Card that last push that had landed their old friend a gorgeous wife. But that situation had been different. Three Card and Renée had had a history. They'd been together before and now they were together again.

Zack and Kim didn't have history. Hell, they didn't have anything beyond a month-long blip in their lives.

"Back off," he said quietly.

"Okay," Hula said, leaning back into a patch of shade thrown by the roof of the old house. "What happens to the doc when you go back into the field?"

"What d'ya mean?"

The other man shrugged. "I mean, if she's in danger still, what'll her old man do? Assign another SEAL to keep watch?"

Everything inside Zack tightened until he thought he just might break apart and the pieces go spinning off into space. Another SEAL? He hadn't thought of that. Hadn't considered it. Of course her father would pull some strings and get someone else to protect her. Of course there'd be another man assigned to this house.

To Kim.

His hand on the beer bottle clenched spasmodically until his fingers ached and he thought he might have felt the glass shatter. His brain got busy. Drawing up images designed to torture him. Another man, some faceless navy man, pitching his seabag into this house, making himself comfortable, sleeping in the tiny room that had been his when Zack had first come here. That same son of a bitch would flirt with Kim, accompany her on her long walks along the river. Maybe take her diving or out on her boat. *He'd* be the one to see her last thing every night and first thing every morning. *He'd* be the one to stand between Kim and danger. *He'd* be the one she turned to when she was scared.

Zack's heartbeat thundered in his ears.

His breath caught in his lungs, frozen until he saw black dots fly in front of his eyes and was forced to draw in air again. His back teeth ground together and a skim of pure fury danced along his bloodstream.

Some nameless, faceless bastard was going to be moving into the bungalow, taking his place. The place he belonged. The one place in the whole world he wanted to be.

How the hell was he supposed to live with that?

Hula chuckled and drew a sharp, steely-eyed

glare from Zack. "Oh, yeah," the man said, with a slow shake of his head, "who said anything about love?"

"Shut up." Zack snarled and got up to walk off his mad while one of his best friends laughed his ass off.

Kim tried to relax, though it wasn't easy.

Even being here, walking along the riverbank, wasn't easing her mind as it used to. But then how could it, with Zack walking beside her? How could she relax knowing that in a few short days, the man she loved would be walking out of her life?

What she needed was to be able to talk about this, about what she was feeling, about the emptiness that leaped to life inside her whenever she thought of Zack leaving. But there was no one she could go to. She'd never had a lot of girlfriends. She couldn't talk to her brothers about this, and her cousins...well, she didn't know if they'd understand. Besides, a selfish part of her wanted to keep this all to herself, despite the need to talk. Which was totally contradictory, of course, but that didn't seem to matter.

A cool breeze lifted off the water and danced past her, touching her with icy fingers that didn't come close to matching the frigid temperatures around her heart. The river water gleamed black and cold in the starlit sky, with no moonlight to glance off its surface. It looked as dark and empty as her heart felt.

She shoved her hands deeper into her pockets and tipped her face up into the wind. That way at least, if her eyes teared, she'd have an excuse for it.

Beside her Zack sighed, reached out and grabbed her arm. Turning her around to face him, he stared down at her through eyes she could see shone with regrets. A pang twinged in her heart, but Kim tried not to let him see it.

"I'll be reporting to base in three days. From there, I'll be shipping out," he said tightly, and she was so surprised, she would have staggered back if he hadn't been holding on to her.

Not that she didn't know he was leaving. Her heart had been ticking off the days for weeks now. Still, neither of them had mentioned it. Like an unspoken agreement, they'd avoided all talk of what would happen when he left.

Now that it was out there, lying between them like an unscalable wall, Kim steeled herself. "I know."

He tore his gaze from hers and stared out at the river, rushing past them as quickly as the days had flown by. "I don't know where I'll be going," he said, his voice almost lost in the muted roar of the water. "But I do know that it's a good thing for me to be going."

"What?"

He looked at her again and either didn't see the sparks flashing in her eyes or chose to ignore them. "Yeah, really. A SEAL shouldn't be tied down, Doc. Shouldn't leave behind people who might... care for him."

"Is that right?"

"Yeah, that's the way it is."

"And what about Three Card? Isn't he married?"

"Yeah, but..."

"And your father was a SEAL, right?"

"True," he said, and shifted position, like a boxer on the ropes trying to find his balance again.

"So basically what you're saying is that it's better for *you* if no one cares about you."

"Look, Kim," he said, reaching out and grabbing hold of her upper arms. He lifted her up onto her toes and met her gaze with wild, frantic eyes. "I was assigned here. It wasn't supposed to be permanent. I wasn't supposed to be anything more than a bodyguard."

The heat of his hands shot straight through the fabric of her jacket and down into her bones, easing away the chill that had been clinging for days. "And is that all it turned out to be?"

He let her go so abruptly she staggered back. "That's not the point."

"It's exactly the point." Her voice lashed at him like a bullwhip. He winced and she was glad to see it. Just as glad to see the coiled tension snaking through his body. "Do you love me?"

"What?" He swiveled his head and stared at her as though she'd popped a third eye in the middle of her forehead.

Shaken, Kim took a deep breath, huffed it out again and repeated the question, though it cost her. After all, what if he said "no"? "Do you love me?"

"For God's sake, Kim—"

"That's the second time you've actually used my name. I like the sound of it."

"Great. Here it comes again. Come on, *Kim*. I'm taking you home."

She pulled her arm out of his grasp and shook her head. "Not a chance. We're staying right here until we get this said."

His mouth firmed into a thin, straight line and his eyes narrowed dangerously. But that wasn't going to deter her any.

"You've already said enough," Zack told her.

"And you haven't answered my question."

"The answer doesn't matter."

She gasped, stepped up close and jabbed her index finger at his chest. "It matters to *me,* you jerk."

"It shouldn't." Zack grabbed her hand and told himself not to feel the sweet rush of heat that swamped him. "Love doesn't solve problems, Doc. It creates 'em."

"Don't do that," she said, her voice filled with a pain that seemed to reach out for him. "Don't start calling me Doc or darlin' or some other cutesy name in some cowardly attempt to pull back from me."

"Cowardly?" Zack stiffened and his fingers around her hand tightened reflexively. "I'm no coward, *darlin'*. And I say what I mean."

"Oh, for—"

But he wasn't going to be stopped now. If she wanted to have this out, then here was as good a place as any. It had to happen at any rate, and they were fast running out of time. In three days, he'd be back to his life and she'd be moving on with hers without him. Best to get this all said now.

"You really think I'm going to stand here and tell you I love you? How can I do that, Kim? That *would* be cowardly—to say that and then leave."

She flinched. "I didn't mean—"

He let go of her hand and reached for her shoulders again. Even through her jacket and the sweat-shirt beneath, he felt the warmth of her skin and he knew he would be dreaming about her forever. "I'm telling you I *can't* love you. I'm a SEAL. You're a damn heiress. Never the twain shall meet, darlin'. Understand?"

She slammed one balled fist into his midsection and since he hadn't been expecting it, she managed to punch the air out of his lungs. He let her go and she took a step back. While he fought to regain his breath, she snarled at him.

"Are you serious?" She walked a wide, angry circle around him and Zack turned, keeping a wary eye on her. "You don't want me because I'm a Danforth?"

"I didn't say—"

"Yes, you did." She cut him off and held up one hand, warning him to silence. "This is amazing," she muttered thickly as her long, inky black hair was lifted by the wind to twist around her head like snakes, each of them ready to strike him down.

Zack thought about interrupting, but the truth was, he didn't think she'd hear him.

"All my life," she was saying, nailing him with a gaze sharp enough to draw blood, "people have wanted to be near me because of what my family might be able to do for them. Charles wanted to marry me because I'm a Danforth. And now you *don't* want me for the same reason?" She shook her head and scooped her hair back out of her eyes. "This is some kind of cosmic joke or something."

If it was a joke, she wasn't laughing and, damn it, neither was he. He'd never meant to hurt her. Never meant for this to happen. And now that it had, he wasn't sure what to do. "Kim…"

"You just be quiet." Her voice broke and that tore at him.

He hadn't really looked at it from her perspective. And now that he had, he could see that by trying to keep from hurting her, he'd brought her pain anyway. Chuck had wanted her money. Zack *didn't* want her money. So from where she was standing, both men had looked at her family's bank accounts rather than at her.

He didn't really care if her name was Danforth or Jones. Behind him, the river rushed on, slapping at its banks, murmuring like a disapproving crowd.

She finally stopped stalking him and when she did, she fired him a look that would have fried a lesser man. Zack figured she was due some temper, so he met her gaze steadily.

"One question, Sheridan," she said, her lips hardly moving, her voice no more than a low murmur. "Do you love me?"

His heart fisted in his chest, became a ball of ice. His lungs strained for air and his hands ached to grab her, hold her. For the first time in his life, he was really in love. The forever kind that he'd never expected to find. But instead of giving in to his own wants, he avoided her question by saying, "I'm a bad risk, Kim."

"You idiot," she said, the curve of her mouth taking the sting out of the words. "Loving somebody is a risk. It means that you're willing to take a chance that will make everything else in the world worthwhile."

The ice around his heart cracked a little and was almost painful. Willing? Hell, his whole life had been a series of calculated risks. Could he really cheat himself out of what might be by refusing to take the biggest risk of all? No, he couldn't. "You sneaked up on me, Kim."

She stiffened slightly, braced herself and asked, "What's that mean, exactly?"

He sucked in air, blew it out and taking his first risk, stepped closer to her. She was awesome. She was strong and brave and willing to risk her own pride for the chance at love. How could he do any less? And how had he ever thought he could live without her?

Zack looked at her and knew he'd been a dead man for nearly a month. He'd been hers the moment she'd opened her front door and fired her first sarcastic shot. She made him laugh, made him think, made his skin sizzle and pop with a single look.

She was everything.

And he had to have her.

He chanced the fury still flashing in her eyes and rested his hands on her shoulders. "It means that I never meant to love you."

Kim swayed a little, then locked her knees to stay upright. She stared into his blue eyes and even in the darkness, she saw the gleam of something warm and wonderful in their depths. Her heartbeat quickened and fluttered in her ears like dozens of birds lifting off the ground at once.

Shaking his head, he admitted, "One look into those grass-green eyes of yours and I was a goner. And still I fought it. I fought against loving you every day since the moment we met."

"Gee, thanks."

"It wasn't easy, darlin'. You're a hell of a temptation." He smiled and moved his hands to cup her face. "I never counted on you, Doc. Hadn't thought a pair of green eyes could slam into me and make me think about white picket fences and home and hearth."

She swayed into him, couldn't help it. The light in his eyes, the smile on his face all combined to make her knees do a slow, lovely melt.

"And kids?" she asked, one corner of her mouth quirking.

"God yes," he said, chuckling. "Kids, too."

Kim's breath slid from her on a sigh of pleasure. She reached up and covered his hands with her own. "I fought against loving you, too, you know. You weren't exactly in my plans."

"Yeah?" he grinned.

Kim's heart turned over, as it would for that smile for the next fifty or sixty years. "Yeah."

"So you love me, huh?" he asked.

"I asked first," she reminded him and felt as if the stars were shining down from Heaven just for them.

"So you did," he said, nodding. "I do love you, Kim Danforth."

She smiled up at him. "That didn't hurt, did it?"

He grinned. "Not so much. I think I could get used to saying it."

She hugged the words to her, knowing she would always remember the very first time he'd said them. "Glad to hear it, because I love you, too, Zack Sheridan."

"God, Kim," he whispered.

Then he pulled her close, wrapping his arms around her, pressing her tightly to him as if half afraid she might try to escape him. But Kim wasn't going anywhere. She'd finally found the one place she wanted to be.

"So," he said against the top of her head, his breath ruffling her hair. "We've got three days left before I ship out."

Her so-full heart gave a little twinge, but she told herself that it was just something she'd have to get used to. Saying goodbye to the man she loved—and looking forward to being reunited. She'd be a good military wife, she thought. He'd never see her cry. He'd never feel her worry. All he would feel was her love. Always.

"And..."

He pulled back so he could see her eyes. "What do you say to a quick Vegas wedding and a two-day honeymoon?" He winked and promised, "I want to be married to you, Kim. And I don't want to wait. We won't have much time together now, but I swear, we'll make every minute count."

"Vegas?" Would he never stop surprising her?

He shrugged and grinned again, and Kim knew she'd go anywhere with him.

"It worked for Three Card," he said.

An elopement, just the two of them. What could be more romantic?

"Then it'll work for us." Kim reached up, grabbed his face and pulled him down for a brief, hard kiss. She couldn't even remember what her life had been like before this amazing man had crashed into it. A Danforth getting married in Vegas. Oh, she couldn't wait to tell the family. "What're we waiting for?"

"Atta girl," Zack said, grabbing her hand and heading for her house. "Oh, and just so you know, if you still need protecting while I'm gone, I'm sending one of my friends to watch over you."

"Another SEAL?" she asked on a laugh, hurrying her steps to keep up with his long-legged stride.

"Oh, no way." Zack stopped suddenly, pulled her into his arms for a brief, rib-crushing hug and then gave her a lopsided smile that stopped her heart. "Not a chance, peaches. From here on out, I'm the only SEAL in your life, got it?"

The only SEAL.

The only man.

The only love she would ever need.

"Hoo-yah."

* * * * *

Don't miss the next books in the
DYNASTIES: THE DANFORTHS *series,*
Sin City Wedding *by Katherine Garbera*
and Scandal Between the Sheets
by Brenda Jackson, available in March.

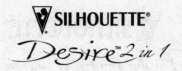

❤ SILHOUETTE®

Desire™ 2 in 1

is proud to introduce

DYNASTIES: THE DANFORTHS

Meet the Danforths—a family of prominence...
tested by scandal, sustained by passion!

Coming Soon!
Twelve thrilling stories in six 2-in-1 volumes:

0105/SH/LC96

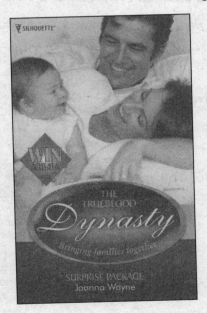

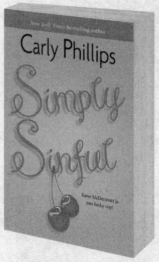

2 FREE

BOOKS AND A SURPRISE GIFT!

We would like to take this opportunity to thank you for reading this Silhouette® book by offering you the chance to take TWO more specially selected titles from the Desire™ series absolutely FREE! We're also making this offer to introduce you to the benefits of the Reader Service™—

- ★ FREE home delivery
- ★ FREE gifts and competitions
- ★ FREE monthly Newsletter
- ★ Exclusive Reader Service offers
- ★ Books available before they're in the shops

Accepting these FREE books and gift places you under no obligation to buy, you may cancel at any time, even after receiving your free shipment. Simply complete your details below and return the entire page to the address below. You don't even need a stamp!

YES! Please send me 2 free Desire books and a surprise gift. I understand that unless you hear from me, I will receive 3 superb new titles every month for just £4.99 each, postage and packing free. I am under no obligation to purchase any books and may cancel my subscription at any time. The free books and gift will be mine to keep in any case.

D5ZED

Ms/Mrs/Miss/Mr ....Initials ....

BLOCK CAPITALS PLEASE

Surname ....

Address ....

....

....Postcode..

Send this whole page to:
UK: FREEPOST CN81, Croydon, CR9 3WZ